Fair

Welcome to Harlequin's great new series, created by some of our bestselling authors from Down Under:

THE AUSTRALIANS

Twelve tales of heated romance and adventure— guaranteed to turn your ~~...~~ down!

Travel to an ~~...~~ ne glamour of th~~...~~ nts of Sydney whe~~...~~ ng women, all feis~~...~~ their biggest challenge yet...falling in love.

And it will take some very special women to tame our heroes! Strong, rugged, often infuriating and always irresistible, they're one hundred percent prime Australian male: hard to get close to...but even harder to forget!

The Wonder from Down Under:
where spirited women win the hearts of
Australia's most independent men.

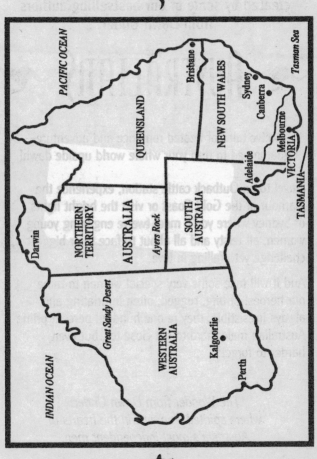

PACIFIC OCEAN

Brisbane

QUEENSLAND

NEW SOUTH WALES

Tasman Sea

Sydney
Canberra

Melbourne
VICTORIA

TASMANIA

Adelaide

SOUTH
AUSTRALIA

AUSTRALIA

Ayers Rock

NORTHERN
TERRITORY

Darwin

Great Sandy Desert

WESTERN
AUSTRALIA

Kalgoorlie

Perth

INDIAN OCEAN

THE
AUSTRALIANS

HER OUTBACK MAN

Margaret Way

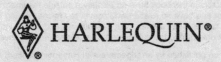

TORONTO • NEW YORK • LONDON
AMSTERDAM • PARIS • SYDNEY • HAMBURG
STOCKHOLM • ATHENS • TOKYO • MILAN • MADRID
PRAGUE • WARSAW • BUDAPEST • AUCKLAND

ISBN 0-373-82579-X

HER OUTBACK MAN

First North American Publication 1999.

Copyright © 1998 by Margaret Way, Pty. Ltd.

Printed in U.S.A.

Margaret Way takes great pleasure in her work and works hard at her pleasure. She enjoys tearing off to the beach with her family on weekends, loves haunting galleries and auctions and is completely given over to French champagne "for every possible joyous occasion." Her home, perched high on a hill overlooking Brisbane, Australia, is her haven. She started writing when her son was a baby, and now she finds there is no better way to spend her time.

CHAPTER ONE

VAST as the homestead was, everywhere Dana looked
there were people; in the drawing room, the library,
Logan's study, the entrance hall of grand dimensions,
even the broad verandas that surrounded the marvellous
old homestead on three sides were crowded with mourners. There must have been four hundred at least. They
had been arriving since early morning in their private
planes and their charter planes set down like a flock of
birds on the station's runway, or in the small army of
vehicles that had made the long hot trek overland; all of
them come to pay their last respects to James Tyler
Dangerfield, second son of this powerful and influential
landed family, dead at twenty-eight, killed in a car crash
after a wild all-night party. Not many people would
know that. Logan, as always, had taken charge very
swiftly, gathering them all in, issuing a brief statement
to the press, making all the arrangements while the entire
Dangerfield clan, pastoralists, judges, scientists and poli-
ticians, one a Government minister, closed ranks behind
him.

Logan was the cattle baron. As direct descendant of
the Dangerfield founding father in colonial Australia, he
was head of one of the country's richest families and
Chairman of the Dangerfield pastoral empire and a network of corporations since the death of his late father,
Sir Matthew Dangerfield some two years earlier. Jimmy
had been the playboy, the second son, forever doomed
to walk in Logan's tall shadow. Logan was the *real*
Dangerfield, Jimmy had often said, never quite able to
conceal his envy and a kind of half-bitter, half-wry re-

sentment at his being second best. Jimmy, with his easy, happy-go-lucky charm, spoiled by the family fortune. Logan was the chip off the old block. The son with unlimited skills and matchless energies. Sir Matthew had worshipped Logan, Jimmy had told her, and Dana had seen that with her own eyes. It had always been perfectly obvious Jimmy could never hope to measure up to his big brother.

Stepbrother.

Logan's mother, Elizabeth Logan Dangerfield, had died giving him birth, something that would not have happened had she elected to have her firstborn in hospital instead of on historic Mara Station to please her husband. Matthew Dangerfield had married Jimmy and Sandra's mother, Ainslie, a few years later, a marriage as nearly a business merger as the first one had been an ecstatic romance. Both Jimmy and Sandra favoured their mother's side of the family, with their golden-brown colouring. Logan was all dark, dangerous Dangerfield, which was to say, unfairly endowed with all of Nature's attributes.

Her expression bleak, Dana turned away from the elegant white wrought-iron balcony to look over to where Logan stood, perhaps on this awful day a little stiffly, his head characteristically thrown up but in perfect control of his emotions as was expected of the head of the family.

Logan, strikingly handsome in his formal dark clothes relieved only by the immaculate white of his shirt, thick blue-black hair, a piercing regard, not that "piercing" fully described the beauty of his sapphire eyes, at six-three, towering over the people around him, a lean and splendid physique. One might have thought it unnecessary to endow him with other qualities, but he had a razor-sharp intelligence he never bothered to conceal and a natural air of command; a capacity for leadership he hadn't developed but had been born with. If there were scores of people who adored Logan Dangerfield, scores more *women,* Dana wasn't one of them. She and Logan looked on one another with a mixture of feelings. Liking wasn't one of them. In the six years since she had first met him they had maintained an uneasy and often electric truce.

The thing was, she would never have moved into his rarified world if it weren't for Melinda. Melinda was her cousin, orphaned child of her mother's sister. Melinda's parents had been killed in a train accident when Melinda was eight and Dana six, and Dana's mother had insisted Melinda come to them. Pretty as a picture, blond-haired and blue-eyed, strangely no one else in the family had wanted her, so Melinda arrived. More than a cousin, a sister, settling into the house as softly and quietly as a little cat. Dana knew better than anyone all about Melinda.

When they were at University, Melinda, two years ahead of eighteen-year-old Dana, had met the Golden Boy, Jimmy Dangerfield, a playboy even then. Jimmy was studying for a degree in Commerce, though he cared little for study. Jimmy was a "dabbler" with no interest in getting on with his work yet he had a perfectly good brain. Something he apparently liked to keep to himself. But Jimmy always had all the money he needed. He got to all the parties and he always had the pretty girls. Jimmy thought being serious about anything was dull and boring. When it was all said and done, all he wanted out of life was fun.

He hadn't really wanted Melinda, though his roving eye had singled out her soft, seemingly vulnerable prettiness. He had taken her out for a time without the slightest awareness of what Melinda was really like. Melinda had an overriding ambition in life. To find *security.* No doubt a consequence of her early traumas. Not the security that mattered, but *money* above all else. Golden Boy Dangerfield was the beginning and end of her search. Known for his love of freedom, Melinda had set Jimmy a trap. She deliberately got herself pregnant, feeling no guilt when Jimmy was forced into a marriage he didn't want, though to his everlasting credit he recognised his responsibilities to Melinda and his coming child. This child was a Dangerfield. He would never have been forgiven had he turned his back on her. Melinda was pretty, intelligent, and from a respectable background. Jimmy had believed she loved him passionately. It wasn't long into the marriage before Jimmy found out she didn't.

Melinda.

At this moment she was lying supposedly sedated in one of the upstairs bedrooms, unable to attend the service, which had been held in the old two-storeyed stone chapel some distance from the homestead, or see her young husband laid to rest on Eagle's Ridge, the family plot surrounded by a six-foot-high wrought-iron fence with ornate double gates. Melinda wasn't prostrate from grief. Dana knew that for a fact. Melinda needed to hide away from all the condemnatory eyes. Dana, who had had a lifetime of fronting for Melinda, was acutely aware of all the subterranean surges and the long speculative glances levelled at her. Everyone knew who she was just as they knew "Tyler's" marriage had not been a happy one. Inevitable some would say when it had started out so badly.

Dana couldn't bear to look back on those days. The image of Melinda, her face paper-white, blue eyes blazing, smiling at her in a sort of conspiratorial triumph.

"He doesn't really want to but I pulled it off, didn't I? He's going to marry me. I'll be a Dangerfield. I'll be rich and important. Mara is *famous*."

Dana then as now felt a sick dismay but she had little

room in her heart for condemnation. Melinda's dream
had turned to ashes. Jimmy had been laid to rest. Life
might have been very different for both of them had
Melinda been more a woman of heart and mind. Going
over to visit them mostly for Alice's, her beloved little
goddaughter's sake had been like going onto a battle
ground. Jimmy had not finished his degree any more
than Melinda had. After an initial period of trying,
Jimmy had quickly settled back into having a good time
while Melinda, to everyone's horror, turned into a shrew,
complaining bitterly to anyone who would listen, having
Alice had caused her to miss out on her youth. Small
wonder Alice growing up in such a household was as
troubled a child as she could be. Dana was her refuge
and they both knew it. Dana could never abandon Alice.
Especially *now*.

What to do with the pain? Dana thought. What to do
with the pain?

She knew Logan blamed her for lots of things, but he
had only said it once. The night of the wedding. The
first time she had ever laid eyes on John Logan
Dangerfield.

CHAPTER TWO

THIS wedding was different. He had known instinctively something was wrong when Tyler came home crowing with delight he had fallen love and wanted to get married immediately.

"She's my blond enchantress," he told them, shocking Ainslie, who had different plans for her son. "I've never met anyone like her. So cool and clever."

It didn't fit the description of the young woman who later flew in to meet them with her coy almost cloying prettiness and shy downcast eyes. The disturbing beauty and the cool intelligence belonged to her cousin. He could never understand how Tyler had looked beyond Dana until it all became clear. But on that day Tyler had his eyes firmly set on Melinda, his young wife, soon to be the mother of his child. Logan had managed to get that out of his beleaguered brother almost at once, backing Tyler's wish to have a quiet wedding on the station attended by family and a few close friends; something that upset Melinda terribly. She had wanted a big wedding with all the trimmings, but the family took no notice of that. It was, after all, a marriage that had been manipulated from the start. But in all fairness, though bitterly disappointed, Ainslie had arranged a wedding pageant and they all did their level best, about fifty in all, to make it a festive occasion. The bride wore virginal white, a soft flowing dress cut to skim the waistline, her pale face hidden by her veil; the cousin wore the same sort of fabric, silk chiffon, he later learned, but in a frosted gold, the bodice leaving her shoulders bare, the long skirt billowing from a small cinched waist. Like the bride, she carried an exquisite bouquet of roses from Mara's home gardens combining all the creams and yellows and golds...

He had been caught up on one of the outstations all morning. The manager there had been foolish enough to try to make a bit extra for himself periodically selling off a few head of prime cattle, so he had to attend to that, a rough confrontation out in the bush, flying back into Mara just over an hour before the ceremony in the family chapel was due to begin. He had never felt less like attending a wedding in his life, knowing Ty, for all his efforts to put on a good face, wasn't happy and he himself was deeply uncomfortable with the idea the bride wasn't just a kitten-faced innocent caught up in an all too common situation but a first-rate opportunist. The cousin she had lived with from childhood was probably the same. He had left before the cousin's flight was due in. She had paid for her ticket to the domestic terminal herself. Something that had surprised him. Melinda had taken to being "looked after" like a duck to water.

Feeling strung out and dishevelled, he had entered the house at the precise moment a young woman in a beautiful strapless gown set her foot on the first landing of the central staircase. She was young, very young, perhaps eighteen or nineteen, but her expression as she looked down at him was one of dignity and maturity.

Tyler's *enchantress,* he thought in one revelatory second, while something hot and hostile flared behind his rib cage.

"You must be Logan," she said sweetly, an answering heat in her flush. "I'd heard you'd been called out."

Her voice, too, was alluring and he gave himself a moment to level out. "To one of our outstations, as it happens." He didn't smile, the formality of his tone in sharp contrast to her natural warmth. "And you must be

Dana?'' Stupid. Of course she was Dana. The cousin.
Yet he couldn't quite believe it. She was blond, like
Melinda, but an ash-blond, very nearly platinum, her
long, thick, straight hair caught back from her face with
a sparkling diadem and allowed to fall down her back.
But where one might have expected Melinda's white
skin and blue eyes, this girl's skin gleamed ivory, her
eyes set in a slight upward slant like the wings of her
eyebrows, velvet brown. It was a stunning combination.

What was even more stunning was the fact he was
staring, but her physical beauty seized his imagination.
Woman magic. A quality that could bring great joy or
havoc or both in equal measure.

She hesitated, perhaps baffled and a little alarmed at
his attitude, while sunlight from the high arched case-
ments lent a startling radiance to her hair and her gown.
He almost felt like calling out, ''Come down, I won't
bite you,'' when she suddenly descended the stairs in
cool challenge, holding up the folds of her skirt with one
hand, the other outstretched towards him.

''How do you do, Logan,'' she said with the utmost
composure. ''I'm so pleased to meet you at last. Jimmy
speaks of you all the time.''

Jimmy. Who was *Jimmy?* To the family, he was Tyler.
He knew from the glitter in her velvet eyes she was
suddenly angry, as hostile in her fashion as he was. Even
the brief contact of hands sent out warning signals as if
to say we may never be open about it but we will never
be friends.

Friends with this young woman? One might as well
be friends with some creature who wrought spells. The
danger was plain. He felt a powerful urge to question
her, to try to get to the bottom of what had happened to
his brother, only it was all too late.

''Please *don't,*'' she said, surprising him, her upturned
face betraying a certain anguish. *Guilt?*

"I'm sorry. I don't follow," he lied, every nerve jangling.

"I think you do." She took a little breath. "We both want Jimmy to be happy."

His voice when it came was so sharp it was like he had splinters in his throat. "You speak of *Tyler* as though you know him very, very well."

Something flickered in her eyes and she flushed as if knowing he had insulted her. "Jimmy is my friend." Still she remained controlled. "I have a warm feeling towards him as befitting someone who is to marry my cousin. I don't want to see him hurt. Melinda, either."

That touched a raw spot. "Are you suggesting *I* do?"

She half turned away from him so he could see her delicate winging shoulder-blades above the low back of her gown. For a moment disconcerted and thoroughly on edge, he felt a strange piercing tenderness for her youth, her beauty, and the fact he had offended her.

"I can look behind your words," she said. "I can see into your eyes. You're upset about the whole situation. Your family, too."

"Well you would know better than anybody how it all came about." He answered too harshly but he was unable to prevent himself.

Her eyes went very dark. "*I* had little part to play in it."

"Well you know," he retorted crisply. "You fit the role of enchantress."

She managed to appear genuinely bewildered. "Why ever are you saying *that*?"

"When Tyler came home he told us he'd fallen hopelessly in love with a *blond enchantress*."

Her delicate brows rose. "Melinda *is* very pretty."

"So she is, in a conventional way," he replied bluntly. "You on the other hand have a quite different look."

Her expression gained a dismayed intensity. "You surely can't think Jimmy and I shared a romance?"

"I'm sure you dazzled him." He smiled at her, looking very dangerous and powerful, but that simply didn't occur to him.

She appeared, for her part, appalled. Perhaps she was. At being found out. "We simply didn't move in the same circles. I barely knew Jimmy until Melinda started going out with him."

"This isn't actually how she tells it." He didn't quite know *how* Melinda was telling it, but she had certainly thrown out lots of veiled hints.

One of the girl's hands fluttered to her breast. She looked for a moment enormously vulnerable. "I can't imagine what Melinda said, but I assure you you've misinterpreted it. This is ridiculous."

"Yes it is." His tone was laced with irony. "Especially as my brother is to marry your cousin in—" he lifted an arm and glanced at his watch "—under an hour. What I really have to do is shower and change. We can talk again."

The chapel was luminous with white flowers, roses, lilies, carnations, stephanotis, great clouds of baby's breath literally transforming it into a fairyland. The bride and her attendant looked as lovely as anyone could wish, the reception in the homestead's ballroom was sumptuous, but hectic circles of colour burned on the bridegroom's cheeks and Logan had to tell him very quietly he was drinking too much.

"Nerves, J.L.! It's not every day a man finds himself married."

Ainslie and Sandra quietly cried into lace-edged handkerchiefs. On the air was a kind of sulphur, like after a thunderstorm. The happy couple, Melinda *did* appear radiant, were to leave on the first leg of their honeymoon

journey that would take them to Europe, only at the very
last minute Tyler pulled their bridesmaid to him and
kissed her full on the lips with a kind of mad jubilation.
Something that made Dame Eleanor Dangerfield turn to
Logan with consternation on her imperious old face. The
girl, Dana the cousin, had made a singularly good im-
pression on her, but what in the world was *that* all about?

Logan faced Dana with it hours later when the household had finally settled. He caught her hand, risking
those warning tingles, drawing her into his study and
shutting the door. "I have to be gone fairly early in the
morning, Dana, so I'll say my goodbyes now. Your charter flight has been arranged for 1:00 p.m. I've taken the
liberty of securing you your on-going ticket. You'll find
it waiting for you at the terminal."

"I didn't want you to do that," she protested, as much
on edge as he was.

"Nevertheless I have. My pleasure. Everything went
off very well."

"It was a beautiful ceremony and the reception was
superb. I must tell you Melinda and I are very apprecia-
tive of everything you've done. She was too emotional
to begin to tell you."

"Perhaps she was marvelling at that kiss Tyler gave
you just as they were leaving?" he said in a tone, half
silk, half steel.

Colour stained her cheeks. "Tyler scarcely knew what
he was doing."

"My God, the rest of us did." Now came the hard
irony.

"Please, Logan, don't you see Jimmy was full of
emotion?" she appealed to him

"I actually thought he was begging you to go with
him." This was disastrous, but he couldn't stop.

"So it's not a marriage made in heaven—" her voice

rang with pain "—but we've got to give it every chance."

He could only marvel at her stricken look. "So what does this involve?" he taunted her. "Do you plan to move out of their lives?"

She looked at him aghast. "Melinda and I are very close. We were reared as sisters."

"But Tyler fell in love with *you* first?" Anyone would.

"Tyler never fell in love with me at all." She shook her head in a kind of desperation.

"Are you sure of that?" The disbelief was thick in his voice.

"Where and when did you learn differently?" she challenged, her eyes sparkling brilliantly, a pulse in her throat at full throttle.

He shifted his gaze unwilling to admit he, too, felt her power. "You must know it shocked a lot of people seeing Tyler reach for you?"

"He wanted comfort." She dropped her head in seeming defeat, but on pure reflex he tilted her chin.

"My dear girl, he had just married your cousin. A very sweet girl. I think *now* Tyler was on the rebound from you. Melinda did tell us he was spellbound by your beauty. I don't know whether you realise it, but your cousin has a problem with you. Sibling rivalry it's called."

"And you'd know a great deal about that yourself." She pushed his hand away, anger lilting out of her voice. "As much as I care about Melinda, she talks a great deal of nonsense at times."

"You don't mind her going off with Tyler?" Better, far better, he shut up, but he couldn't.

"All I want for them is to be happy."

"Well, *good*," was his sardonic answer. "I don't want to have to worry about you, to tell the truth."

"Worry about *me?*" She spun so the long flowing skirt of her dress flared out around her.

It came to him with amazement his own emotions were surging dangerously. "You must see it will be better for you to get on with your life."

Again her face flamed. "If I weren't stuck in the middle of the Never-Never I'd be out of here in a second."

"Forgive me." He could hear the ringing arrogance in his apology. "You are a guest in my home."

"And you're a very powerful and dangerous man," she said, looking out at him accusingly from her great dark eyes. "It hasn't just occurred to me. I've listened to everything Jimmy has said about you."

His downward stare was more daunting than he knew. "Tyler loves me as I love him," he said coldly. "I know he has his hangups—who doesn't?—but he knows he can always count on my support."

"Surely that's to be expected of a brother?" Her scorn was genuine.

"And what can be expected of cousins?" he countered harshly. "Cousins as close as *sisters?*"

Her slender body fairly danced with fury mixed up with a kind of anguish that showed in her eyes. He saw the bright flash in them, like a flame set to oil, then she brought up her hand incredibly to strike him. He couldn't for the life of him think why, but it made him want to laugh. He hadn't seen such spirit for ages. He caught her hand in mid-flight, his own blood aflame, then for one extraordinary never-to-be-repeated moment swept her into his arms, covering her romantic soft mouth in a kiss so raw and ruthless it later filled him with a kind of horror and self-contempt. For all her beauty and female allure she was little more than a schoolgirl.

She didn't speak afterwards, as shocked as he was and close to tears. He knew he had to keep hold of her all the time he was apologising, his senses swimming and his veins continuing to run lava. He knew she would never forgive him and God knows he had his own intense forebodings about her. Certain women because of their female power and seductiveness could bring destruction to a family.

Ainslie's long distinguished face was distorted with grief. Dana's heart ached for her but she knew from the outset Ainslie wanted no words of sympathy from her.

"That dreadful girl," Ainslie moaned, her fine skin mottled with red. "I knew the moment I laid eyes on her she would bring grief to this family."

What matter now? Dana had thought it herself. Still she tried to defend her cousin, so ingrained with the habit. "Ainslie, Melinda is bereft. We're full of anguish. It's so dreadfully, dreadfully tragic."

"Ah don't defend her, Dana," Ainslie admonished her. "No more. We women can't fool one another. There's something twisted about my daughter-in-law. Look how she is with poor little Alice. She never loved my son, either. Why couldn't *you* have been the one?"

Dana couldn't hide her shock. "But it wasn't that way, Ainslie. Jimmy had no romantic feelings towards me."

"Tyler *loved* you," Ainslie said, sounding utterly convinced.

Dana laboured hard to correct her. "As a friend. A *good* friend."

"No, my dear." Ainslie gave her a small, sad smile. "He told me he loved you."

"Jimmy did?" Dana's shock was total.

Ainslie sighed heavily, patting Dana's hand. "Please don't call him Jimmy in my presence, dear."

Dana flushed with dismay. "Forgive me but it's what—Tyler called himself. The very last thing I want to do is upset you, Ainslie. What Tyler *meant* was, he loved me as family. Alice's godmother.''

Ainslie looked obliquely at her, drying her deeply shadowed eyes. ''You're much too intelligent and intuitive a young woman to say that. Tyler admired as well as loved you. Surely you know Melinda was sick with jealousy?''

Dana set her jaw against her sudden anger. Anyone who knew Melinda knew she habitually lied. ''That's not possible, Ainslie.'' Dana felt like she was drowning in deception. ''Believe me on this terrible day when I say there was nothing between Tyler and me but a deep friendship. I was his confidante when—''

''When things got bad with Melinda,'' Ainslie interrupted. ''I know. Tyler told me. In those early days I prayed and prayed the marriage would work. But I hadn't reckoned on what Melinda was really like. She planned her pregnancy to trap my son.''

''But we have Alice, don't we?'' Dana pointed out with great gentleness.

''Yes, we have Alice.'' Ainslie gave a shuddering sigh. ''We have no choice but to go on, but I don't want to be near Melinda today, Dana. I don't think anyone else does, either. It's sad, but that's life. She has always pretended to be so quiet and sweet, yet all the time she's been causing trouble. The marriage would have worked had she really been what she pretended, instead Tyler's gone and we're all punished.''

Sandra was less restrained, off balance with grief and swollen-eyed.

''This is a house of mourning, Dana,'' she cried, her hazel eyes clouded with her inner rage. ''It's a good thing Melinda has chosen to hide away upstairs. I knew last night she was in a panic about fronting up. *You* had to do that for her. I know she's your cousin, but I really think you shouldn't bother with your loyalty anymore. She depends on you, I know, but she's not your friend.''

Hold the presses, Dana thought dismally. It was no news. ''Sandra, don't compound all this grief,'' she warned, leaning forward to kiss Sandra's cheek.

''I'm sorry, Dana, I can't seem to stop. What we should have stopped was the wedding. It was never destined to work out. Look at Alice, the sheer misery of that little girl. You don't think Logan's going to let Melinda take her out of our lives? A cat's a better mother. A cat is kinder.''

Dana took Sandra's hand between her own and rubbed it. It was icy cold. ''Melinda doesn't want to do that. You're Alice's family.''

''We are,'' Sandra replied fiercely, ''so we can't desert her. Melinda has never found a place in her life for Alice. Anyone would think Alice was thrust upon her instead of...''

''Alice is very important to me, as well.'' Dana led the tormented Sandra farther away from the other mourners.

''She loves you. She adores you.'' Sandra nodded her head frantically. ''She wants to belong to you. So did Tyler.''

Dana wanted to protest the truth from the rooftops. ''Sandy, why are you saying this? It makes me sick with dismay. Tyler and I were friends. That was the extent of our relationship. Why are you speaking out like this now? Why the sudden doubts?''

''And Melinda *dreamed* up all the rest?'' Sandra gave a broken laugh.

''I don't want to have to say this, but I must.'' Dana looked back at the other woman very directly. ''Melinda has a gift for twisting the truth.''

''We learned that,'' Sandra confirmed bleakly. ''She was born to breed trouble. I don't think badly of you,

Dana. I can't. You're too honourable and decent. If Tyler loved you, I do, too.''

The crushing burden of misunderstanding was too much for Dana to bear. She withdrew at the first opportunity and went upstairs to Melinda's bedroom, shutting the door behind her and moving over to the huge four-poster bed where her cousin lay her golden head pressed into a mound of pillows.

''Is it *too* ghastly?'' Melinda asked in a sympathetic tone.

Dana felt a powerful tide of revulsion. ''Ghastly, why *wouldn't* it be ghastly? I keep seeing Jimmy striding along the beach holding Alice on his shoulders, both of them laughing. Jimmy, my God, my God, he was only twenty-eight. The family is devastated.''

''That's it. Ignore *me*.''

Dana heard the tremble in Melinda's voice and tried desperately to rein herself in. ''I know your suffering in your way, Melinda.''

''Don't think for a moment I'm not,'' Melinda retorted, admonishing her. She sat up, plumping the pillows behind her. ''And what about you? You look wonderful in black, darling. As though you didn't know,'' she added archly.

Dana shook her head slowly. ''I simply don't understand you, Melinda, and the things you say.''

''Oh, yes, you do.'' Melinda gave a brittle laugh. ''I've never been able to fool you, from day one. Worst of all, in some subtle way you've become my enemy.''

''Ah, cut the act,'' Dana snapped. ''I don't want to listen to your nonsense anymore.''

''It's not an act, I mean it,'' Melinda shouted. ''I bet they all hate me downstairs.''

''Well, you haven't tried very hard, have you?'' Dana all but abandoned herself to her disgust.

"I never did have Jimmy completely to myself, did I?" Melinda said, her voice hard and sullen.

"I know there were other women," Dana said heavily, forced to agree.

"Other women?" Melinda sneered. "The only one who counted was *you*."

"So this is how you mean to play it." Finally Dana saw the light. "Are you never going to stop playing fast and loose with the truth?"

"I'm not going to change," Melinda confirmed. "I saw the way he looked at you. The innocent temptress in our midst."

The colour drained entirely from Dana's face. "Spread that lie and I don't see how you can live with yourself. It's a bid for sympathy, isn't it? You want the family to forgive you. Let you back in. I'm to be the scapegoat. The marriage couldn't work because *I* came between you both. It won't wash, Melinda. *You* know it. *I* know it. The only feeling I had for Jimmy was friendship."

Melinda gave a bitter laugh. "You've always been too good to be true. I really can't help what anyone else thinks. They didn't get it from me. Jimmy was the stupid one. He opened his big mouth. You know Logan hates you."

Dana pulled back from the bed like it had caught fire. "He does not. We mightn't be compatible but he doesn't hate me."

"He does, too," Melinda confirmed as though she'd just heard it straight from Logan's mouth. "I'm amazed you refuse to believe it. Logan's ten times the man Jimmy was, but *you* couldn't catch him in a million light-years." There was a glitter of pure malice in Melinda's blue eyes.

Dana's breath came so hard she nearly choked.

"Catch him? Aren't you mixing me up with someone else?"

At that, Melinda's cheeks burned. "You've been dying to say that all these years, haven't you?"

"It would never have helped anyone to have said it," Dana answered bluntly. "Be warned, I'm not going to allow you to make up lies about me, Melinda. And about Jimmy. I can't help what Logan thinks. You must be some sort of a monster. I've done everything I could to support you since we were kids."

"I know. You're a bred-in-the-bone do-gooder," Melinda replied almost cheerfully with her odd capacity to confound. "Logan thinks it was good old you who first captured Jimmy's heart. Which you did. But it was *later,* and all unaware. I used to watch the two of you together and enjoy a good laugh. Jimmy knew you would never look at him. Then you got engaged to your precious Gerard. What a swathe you two cut. You so blond, he so dark. Both of you so damned clever. You never did tell me what happened there."

"I couldn't love Gerard in the way he wanted," Dana said in a voice as quiet as possible. "I realise now it wasn't love. It was deep affection. Gerard deserved the lovely girl he has since married."

"And you're all friends," Melinda crowed. "That's the really funny part. Your lovely friend Lucy is a bit of an idiot if you ask me."

"You can't hurt her, Melinda," Dana said. "You can't hurt Gerard and you can't hurt me, though you've tried often enough."

Melinda's shoulders against the pillows went rigid. "I'm scared, Dana," she suddenly confessed. "I'm so terrified I'm shaking inside. What if Jimmy changed his will?"

Dana caught the panic in her cousin's voice. "You think he did?"

"Well, he didn't love me, darling." Melinda was back to mockery.

"He might have had you given him a chance. He never mentioned anything about changing his will to me. You are his widow."

"And Alice was his dear little changeling. How she ever got to be so plain I'll never know. I've been complimented on my looks all my life. Jimmy was very good-looking. Not like Logan, of course, but then, who the hell is?"

"Alice will come into her own as she matures," Dana said sharply, her condemnation of Melinda spilling out. "Ainslie is a distinguished-looking woman. Alice takes after her grandmother."

"With a face like a horse," Melinda said waspishly.

"A *thoroughbred,* that's the thing. It's terrible what you're doing to Alice, Melinda. One day you're going to bitterly regret it. You're starving her of your love."

"I am not and I never have been. I just don't pander to her like you do. In many ways she's a big disappointment to me. You might think of that while you're ticking me off. She's difficult, she's plain, and she doesn't know how to *behave.* I've had to put up with her tantrums for years on end. I've had no life. I lost all that when I married Jimmy. I thought we were going to travel the world staying in the best hotels. But he had to stay close to you and his adored family. Well close enough. No way anyone could expect me to live out here. It's like another planet. Maybe Mars."

"Until it turns into the biggest garden on earth. I must go back, Melinda," Dana said tiredly. It was impossible to get through to her cousin.

"Do that," Melinda called after her bitterly. "Don't forget to give them all my love. I'm sure you've been answering queries about the bereaved widow around the clock."

*   *   *

By late afternoon everyone had left except two elderly relatives who couldn't face the return journey and had elected to retire with a light supper to be served later in their rooms. Ainslie was at the end of her tether and had retired, as well, taking a sedative at the behest of her doctor. Sandra, wishing to escape for a few hours and openly hostile to Melinda, had flown out for the night with her boyfriend, Jack Cordell, and his family. The Cordells owned Jindaroo Station on Mara's north-east border, some sixty miles away. Alice, tired out by her accumulated tears and fears, had for once climbed quietly into her bed and instantly fell into a deep sleep from which she was not to wake until dawn the following morning.

Left to her own devices, Dana sat on the veranda looking over the extraordinary sweeping vista of Mara's home gardens. It never failed to move her how the early settlers through their sense of nostalgia had tried to re-create something of "home" in a landscape as remote from the misty beauty of the British Isles as the far side of the moon, yet the Dangerfields had succeeded to a remarkable degree. Every last mistress of Mara had been a passionate gardener, but it took Ainslie to begin the long task of replacing exotics extremely difficult to get to flourish with the wonderful natives that abounded but had hitherto been considered too "strange."

Dana would never forget her first visit to Mara. Nothing could have prepared her for the heart-stopping sight of a magnificent green oasis in the middle of a red desert. The splendid homestead was sheltered by magnificent old trees planted to mark the birth of each child through the generations. For one family to have established all this was inspiring. Even more incredulous was the garden's dimensions. Fed by underground bores, it included its own huge informal lake with its colony of black swans and wealth of water plants. There were

sunken rose gardens with long beds of massed plantings
and wonderful old statuary brought out from England,
native gardens, fruit gardens and vegetable gardens all
tended by a small army of groundsmen under a Mr.
Aitkinson who had been with the family since forever
and was a horticulturist of some note. Great sheaves of
flowers from Mara's gardens had covered Jimmy's cas-
ket.

At the memory, tears rushed into Dana's eyes and she
stood up, twisting her body as though trying to shake
off a great burden of sadness. She couldn't fully take in
what the family was saying about her and Jimmy. She
would have to make a great effort to remember to call
him Tyler. Certainly they had grown close over the
years, their love and concern for Alice their common
bond, but to suggest Jimmy had loved her in any romantic sense simply wasn't true. He had never shown a
hint of it in his behaviour. Indeed he had treated her
more like a sister with a tender affection. Was it possible
she had been blinded by her own immunity? Had she
failed to divine his true feelings?

It was an unhappy fact Jimmy had turned to other
women for comfort and sexual release. Melinda, so eager
for his lovemaking before their marriage, had inexplicably turned off physical intimacy after the birth of their
child. Or so Jimmy had thought. Dana knew her cousin
better. Even as a child Melinda, behind the soft smiles,
had been a cold and manipulative little person. "Grasping" one of Dana's friends had called her. A charge that
had upset Dana at the time but one she was later forced
to admit was impossible to defend. The same friend had
suggested to Dana that her cousin's "love" for her contained an element of deep resentment.

In her heart Dana knew it. There had been many little
betrayals through the years. It was Melinda who had
planted the seed. To cause doubt in them all. To lessen

Dana's standing in the eyes of the family. She was the third person in a doomed relationship. Whatever Melinda's purpose, the strategy had succeeded. Dana had won over Ainslie and Sandra, all three of them naturally compatible, but as for Logan? Logan had distrusted her from day one.

Logan, too, had a failed engagement. Dana had met Phillipa Wrightsman on several occasions although she had not attended the engagement party nor had she been invited. Phillipa, as a member of the landed gentry, was eminently suitable to succeed Ainslie as mistress of Mara. But the engagement hadn't worked. No one seemed to know why. Logan never spoke about it other than to say the decision was mutual. The family wouldn't have it any girl in her right mind would reject Logan. In fact Dana, with her excellent eye, had taken note this very day Phillipa was still in love with her ex-fiancé. Logan had driven Phillipa and her family down to the airstrip some twenty minutes before with Phillipa holding on to Logan's arm. Phillipa had tried to be friendly but Dana knew she would never be regarded as anyone else but Melinda's cousin. Melinda was deeply disliked, although the extended family had tried hard to disguise it in the name of good manners. Melinda's blond curls and big blue eyes had rarely seduced her own sex, either.

Even as Dana stood at the balcony, her hands gripping the wrought-iron railing, a jeep swept through the open gates of the main compound. Logan returning. There was no time to retreat. He brought the jeep to a halt near the central three-tiered fountain, swung out, slammed the door and took the short flight of stone steps to the homestead in two lopes.

If Dana had been asked to sum up Logan Dangerfield with one word it would have been: *electric*. He radiated power. It crackled and flew in the very air around him.

She had never in her life met anyone who could equal Logan for sheer impact and she had met many high-profile people in the course of her work as a professional photographer. Though he would be amazed and not too pleased to hear it, she had a framed photograph of him in her apartment. She had taken it herself, an action shot of him on horseback, controlling his favourite stallion, Ebony King, spooked by a visitor's flyaway hat. It was a great shot. All her girlfriends who saw it thought she had to be madly in love with him. Not really believing her when she said all that had ever been between her and Logan was a kind of cold war. Nothing but that unspeakable, unbanishable kiss. Not a kiss. A punishment.

"You look terribly on edge," Logan now said, his brilliant eyes moving over her with extraordinary intensity yet that curious reserve.

"So do you," she responded tightly, taking a chair.

"God, why not? On this horrendous day." He had removed his suit jacket sometime earlier, now he jerked at his black tie, pulling it off and throwing it over the back of one of the wicker armchairs. "Where's everyone?" He unloosened the top button of his shirt then another, exposing the strong brown column of his throat.

"Ainslie has retired," she told him quietly.

"Poor Ainslie!" His voice was deep with sympathy. "For a mother to lose her son and in such a way. Uncle George and Aunt Patricia? What about them?"

"They're played out. They're having a light supper in their room. Alice is asleep, as well. She's worn out by her tears. It's been a terrible day for her."

"I know." Under his dark copper tan was a distinct pallor. "And Melinda? I have to tell you, Dana, I hope I'm not seeing her tonight. I just couldn't take it."

"She's staying in her room." Dana's voice firmed.

"She said to tell you she'll be taking the plane out in the morning."

"After the will reading, I bet. What about you?" He shot her a quick look. A recent assignment on the Great Barrier Reef had gilded her skin. It glowed like a pale golden pearl against the sombre black of her two-piece suit.

"I'll be going, as well, of course." She looked back at him in consternation.

"I thought you might think of family for once," he replied bitingly. "Ainslie and Sandra. They could do with your company."

"I can't stay here without Melinda, Logan. Surely you see that?"

"No, I *don't*," he clipped off. "The best thing you could do, Dana, is get shot of your cousin."

"And what about Alice?" she retaliated, her own brown eyes suddenly blazing. It was always like this with Logan.

He pulled out a chair and slumped into it moodily. "Yes, yes. Poor little Alice. My heart bleeds for that child. At least when Tyler was there…" He broke off in grief and anger.

"*I'm* here, Logan." Her eyes welled with tears and she turned away abruptly so he couldn't see.

His laugh was discordant. "And we're very grateful for that. Why don't you and Alice stay on for a few days? I'm sure Melinda won't mind. She's let you take care of Alice often enough."

Dana turned, feeling a queer stab of regret. One part of her would have loved to stay but as a fellowship-winning photographer and currently "hot" property on the art scene, she had numerous commitments. "Logan, I'd do what I could," she said, "but I have assignments and a set of pictures for a Sydney showing due in.

Besides, when have you ever wanted me around the place?''

His eyes were as hot and stormy as the electric blue sky. ''Don't be so bloody ridiculous,'' he rasped.

''I'm not being ridiculous at all,'' she retorted, stung by his long-held attitudes. ''You've never liked me, Logan, any more than I like you.''

''So what do you want from me?'' he taunted, deliberately trying to stir her. ''What you're used to? Men who worship the ground you walk upon?''

''If that were true, we'd have an awful lot in common,'' she flared. ''Phillipa is still in love with you.

He looked back dispassionately. ''Like most women, Phillipa doesn't want to let go. She'll meet someone soon.''

''I hope so, for her sake,'' Dana answered, suddenly sounding very cool, though it cost her dearly. ''It's been three years.''

''Really?'' He shifted position abruptly so he could stare at her. Face to face. ''I didn't realise you kept such tabs on me.''

Before she could prevent herself she arched back in her chair, her two hands gripped together. It was a significant move, one he appreciated from the mocking look on his face. ''How could I not know what was happening in your life. I saw Jimmy—''

Logan winced, dangerously close to breaking loose. ''Can't you say Tyler?''

''Of course I can.'' She took a deep breath, trying to hold on to her own escalating emotions. ''But it will take time. Tyler was Jimmy to us. I suppose he was trying for a new life.'' She stopped abruptly, continued in a gentler tone. ''He used to love to talk about you. About Mara. When you were boys. He had such great love for you, Logan. Such respect and admiration.''

His knuckles gripped until they gleamed bone white.

"But I wasn't able to help him at the end?" There was a whole world of regret in it.

"He was a grown man," Dana offered in the spirit of reconciliation, though every nerve in her body was on edge. This had been such a terrible day for everybody. She could see the depth of Logan's grief.

"And he had the great misfortune to marry Melinda. Just about any other girl would have made a go of it." It was said not in anger, more a point of fact.

Dana sighed, a sad and haunted look in her eyes. "Tragically they weren't suited to each other at all." She put back a hand, lifted her long hair away from her hot nape, unaware a beam of sunlight was streaming through it turning it to a waterfall of ash gold. When she looked back at Logan, some expression in his eyes made her heart pound. It wasn't anger or even the sexual hostility that often flared between them, but something more primitive and dangerous. "Is something wrong?" she asked, a betraying tremor in her voice.

He shoved back his chair, stood up, all six foot three, flexing the muscles in his back. No one better than Logan to throw a long shadow. "Sometimes I can't take your feminine wiles," he growled.

She stared up at him in amazement. "I've never met anyone in my life who fires up like you do," she protested. "*What* feminine wiles?"

He shot her a sharp, potent glance. "Hell, every time I see you, you've got a new one. I guess you're the sort of woman a man would do anything to have." There was condemnation mixed up with the grudging admiration.

"Well, I haven't made my mark on you." Dana, in her turn, jumped up from her chair. What *was* this between her and Logan? A kind of love-hate? Nothing else came to mind.

"On the contrary, you made your mark," he said

moodily. "You were dangerous as little more than a schoolgirl," he brooded. "Now you're a woman and ten times more alluring. Ah, what the hell! Let's get away from the house," he said with a kind of urgency. "Change your clothes. We'll ride. I feel like galloping to the very edge of the earth."

CHAPTER THREE

AND gallop he did, with the kind of desperate anguish Dana shared. Though an excellent rider, well mounted, she couldn't hope to match him, but she drove her beautiful spirited mare until her aching head started to clear and the awesome splendour of the sky entered her blood.

A storm was coming. The very air sizzled with the build up of electricity. On the western horizon huge mushrooming clouds of purple and silver were shot with flame as the slanting rays of the sun cut a great swathe through them. Even the sandhills on the desert border glowed like furnaces against the eerie, super-charged sky. It was a barbaric scene and, despite her grief, Dana felt a rising wave of excitement.

Birds, great flights of them, were coming from all points of the compass, splitting the air with their cries. They passed overhead at lightning speed, homing into the shadowy sanctuary of swamps, billabongs and lagoons that crisscrossed the vast landscape. The air vibrated with the whirr of a million brilliantly coloured wings. Often such spectacular atmospheric effects came to nothing or little more than a fine beading of raindrops, but Dana could tell from the violent and acid-green streaks in the heatwaves this was going to be big. She believed wholeheartedly the storm was sent to mark Tyler's passing.

Logan thought so, too. She could see it in his face, dark, brooding, despairing.

"We'd better take shelter," he shouted to her, lifting his voice as the first clap of thunder rolled across the heavens. Even as they turned the horses towards the line of shallow caves the aboriginals called Yamacootra, a jagged spear of lightning flashed through the low canopy of clouds. The caves right in the heart of Mara were prehistoric sites, hallowed ground inhabited by Dreamtime spirits, the largest of them pitched high at the dome allowing easy access to a man as tall as Logan. It was there they headed. Incandescent light seething around them as they galloped up the slope. Once a pair of brolgas shot up from a huge clump of cane grass, causing Dana's mare to rear in sudden fright. So strong was the tension in the atmosphere she thought she would be thrown but Logan closed in on her, grabbing at the reins and subduing the mare with his superior strength.

When they arrived at the entrance Logan settled the excited, sweating horses in an overhang partially screened by high tangled vegetation and a spindly ghost gum growing out of rock. A bank of flowering lantana all but blocked the mouth of the cave but Logan ripped it aside as the driving wind turned the fallen leaves into a whirlwind of green and purple. Temporarily blinded by the whirling cloud Dana lurched over a half-hidden rock, clawing at Logan's shirt to keep her balance.

"Here, steady, I've got you." His strong arm whipped around her and he muffled a violent oath as a disturbed goanna, fully six feet in length, shot out of the cave opening like a projectile, hissing at them hoarsely.

Dana held a hand over her face for protection. Her heart was thudding behind her ribs. Logan was holding her so painfully close she had to grit her teeth against a whole range of electrifying sensations.

Logan shouted at the giant lizard, watching it race down the slope. "Go on, get. I just hope he hasn't got a mate." Shielding her body with his own, Logan entered the cave, his eyes darting swiftly around the interior. There was plenty of light now as brilliant spears of lightning forked down the sky. The ancient stone walls glowed with ochres, red, yellow, burnt orange, black and white and charcoal.

Moving very quietly, Dana moved back into the cave, further unnerved by the presence of little lizards that dashed across the sand at her feet. This wasn't the first time she had been inside the cave. Logan had permitted her access several times, but for once she felt threatened by the forces that were at work all around them. The cave was eerie, hushed, dim except for the brilliant flashes of light. There was hardly an inch of wall and roof space that wasn't covered in drawings of totemic beings and creatures. Like the great undulating coils of the Rainbow Snake executed on ochres, stark white and charcoal. As the lightning flashed, the snake seemed to move, causing Dana an irrational spasm of fear. She continued to move about, trying to cover her agitated state of mind though it must have been obvious to Logan. A great crocodile was incised and painted on the wall, its broad primeval snout peering out of what appeared to be a clump of reeds. A crocodile in the desert? Either the aboriginal artist was a nomad or the drawing dated back to the inland sea of prehistory. In a sort of desperation she stopped and focused on it, murmuring more to herself than Logan who was standing at the entrance of the cave staring out at the brilliant pyrotechnics.

"I'd love to photograph all this. It would sell like hot cakes."

"The answer is no," he threw over his shoulder.

"I understand why."

"That's why you've been allowed in."

"No need to snap my head off." Damn, his tone of voice wasn't the problem. It was being alone with him. Both of them usually took care it didn't happen. He was standing quite still but his whole aura told her he was on full alert. Would she ever find an answer to the mystery that was Logan Dangerfield? The rain was coming down harder now, falling in a solid silver sheet from the overhang. They might have been sealed in some ancient temple.

For the first time she noticed Logan's tanned skin, taut over his chiselled bones, was sheened with rain. His blue-black hair was damp, as well, curling over the collar of his denim shirt. He always wore his thick waving hair full and a little long, not wasting much time looking for hairdressers. He didn't have to. Most women would give anything to have hair like that. Once or twice she had seen him with a beard when he'd been away for weeks on end visiting the outstations. The sight of him *wild* with his blue eyes blazing had all but dried up her mouth. She realised now she had always revelled in his arrogance and splendid male beauty even as she buried it in the wary banter they indulged in.

Another bolt of thunder flashed across the heavens, then a flash of lightning so harsh it was almost withering, filled the cave.

Dana in sheer reaction fell to her knees holding both hands across her ears.

"It's okay." Logan tried to comfort her though he spoke between his clenched teeth. He crossed to her, easing himself down on his haunches. "Dana?"

She didn't answer, her ash-blond head down between her arms. He took a thick silky fistful of hair, lifting her face to him. He had never seen her eyes so huge, so dark, pools of an answering tension. Her body might have been wired it was so electric to his touch. "No need to panic. You've seen a storm before." Even as he spoke his words were almost drowned out by the violent crack of thunder that crashed like a giant drum. There were massive thunder-heads backlit by flashes that rivalled the brilliance of the sun. If the rain kept coming, all the gullies would be overflowing, bringing precious water to the eternally thirsty land. A strong wind had blown up outside the cave, parting the silver curtain of rain so that it flew into the mouth of the cave. They were forced to pull back into the interior. Logan, with one arm, half dragged her across the sand.

Today of all days he thought he could just lose his last hold on control, do something both of them would regret all their lives. But his feeling for her ran contrary to his will. It was an urgent pulse drumming deep inside of him. Desire that had been buried deep since the first time he had taken her in his arms. "Damn you, Dana," he said explosively.

"And damn you, too," Dana answered with equal fervour, trying to break his strong grip. "I can't bear to be with you, Logan."

The knowledge tore at him. "So what are you waiting for?" He jerked her to her feet, overcome by sexual hostility that fairly crackled and spat. "This isn't the biggest storm I've ever seen. In a minute or so it will be all over. You can ride."

That sent her wild. "Why do you hate me?" she hurled at him. "Melinda told me you did but I wouldn't believe it. But it's *true*. You're so cruel. Then I see another side of you. You're so bloody charming, so bloody *perverse!*"

His blue eyes blazed an ominous warning. "I don't hate you, Dana. Far from it. But my heart and mind are locked and barred against you."

"Why?" She cursed herself for asking but she was obsessed with knowing. "Can't you tell me *why?*"

"You've known since the day I met you," he returned harshly. "For what happened between you and Tyler. Melinda wasn't alone in this disaster. *Your* hold on Tyler was too powerful for him to break."

Any sense of balance disappeared entirely. She closed her eyes, shuttering them with her lashes. "What you're saying is terrible. It's so ugly."

"Yes, it *is*," he agreed with terrible irony. "You may not have broken any code of honour but there were consequences, Dana. Consequences for us all. You were forbidden to Tyler, just as you're forbidden to me."

Forbidden? Was that the awful truth? "You're crazy," Dana said in dull despair.

"He told me you were the best thing in his life," Logan said just as bleakly.

"The best thing in his life was *Alice*." Her voice picked up power. "My only role was *friend*. Can't you get that through your fool head?" A dull roaring had begun in her ears. Fool? Logan Dangerfield. What was she saying?

"I don't give a damn for words, Dana."

"You're calling me a liar? I don't like that."

His blue eyes *burned*. "Then how come Tyler spoke so lovingly of you to us all? Ainslie, Sandra, me. Even Alice. You were in all his letters. I can show them to you. Hell, Dana. He was my brother. I understood him."

"He couldn't have said we were *lovers*. He could never have said that," Dana waivered, wondering if she had ever known Jimmy at all.

"*Were* you?" Logan caught her face between his hands, forced her to look at him.

"I would swear on his grave." She was trembling so violently she thought she might fall.

"Do you mean that?" He shook her as though unable to deal with his anger.

"Of course I mean it. Why are you trying to ruin my life? Why are you trying to force this role of seductress on me?"

"Because I have to *know*."

"Why is it so terribly important to you?" she demanded. "You act as if you can't stand it." In another minute she knew she'd either cry or lunge at him.

"Maybe I *can't*." His voice was very bitter. "I knew

the minute you stopped my breath with your beauty you would know how to wreck lives."

She felt ravaged, full of pain. What he was saying was monstrous.

"I want to leave." Dana held up her hand as if to ward off danger.

"I'm not going to stop you," he rasped.

"Because you're afraid. The great Logan Dangerfield, master of all he surveys, is afraid. Afraid of a woman." Hostility flooded her, an aching desire to punish him as he punished her. "You know in your heart there was nothing between Jimmy and me, but you have to tear at me anyway. You know why? Because you don't want to answer to your own desires. It must be really bad for you to want a woman you profess to despise."

It was a moment of such tremendous tension Dana feared a dizzy spell. What was happening was more powerful than either of them. Adrenaline coursed through her overheated veins, so her body flushed. She turned on her heel, determined to rush out into the driving storm, but he came after her, locking a steely arm around her, staring down into her face framed by the blond turbulence of her hair.

"Don't be a damned fool," he said, feeling on this day of all days just touching her would set off a landslide.

"Better the storm than you," Dana cried tempestuously, feeling all the air was being sucked out of her body. Didn't he know his long fingers were cupping her breast?

"Dana, don't do this. *Don't*." His nerves were so jangled his hands were rough, but she continued to struggle as if she didn't care, more invited it. Her struggles and the high soft moans that went with it like a keening bird, only served to inflame him.

Finally he lost it. Lost whatever had held him in check

all these years. Furiously, a driven man, he spun her into
his arms, his mouth moving with insatiable hunger all
over her face, her temples, her eyes, her cheeks, her
breathtaking mouth, her high arched throat, bending her
backwards until he could taste the sweet satin swell of
her breast. He knew he shouldn't give in to this but the
whole catastrophe of the day had shattered him. She was
Dana. She was Woman. She was Fantasy. A liberation
from the black well of grief. He wanted her even if she
detested him.

But Dana, too, was in the relentless grip of passion.
She had always known this man could break her heart.
Hadn't their relationship always been fraught with inten-
sities? She knew she would bitterly regret this. But for
now…for now… In his way he was an irresistible force.
Her body was responding to him like it responded to
nobody else and never would. She realised in a moment
of terrible truth she loved him. That all the emotional
ambiguities had nothing to do with her deepest driven
secret. She wanted him as badly as he wanted her, both
of them wholly dependant on the other to reaffirm Life.

His mouth and the questing urgency of his hands left
her breathless, half crazed. For all they had tried, what
was about to happen could not be averted. It was even
a release to get it out into the open, the dream after
midnight become reality.

She was lying on the sand, feeling its coolness against
her heated skin. She saw Logan bending over her, his
dynamic dark face all taut planes and angles, his blue
eyes blazing like the jewels in some primitive mask.
Hadn't she known in her heart of hearts this was going
to happen? She had hidden from the danger, now she
was mad to embrace it.

But it was all *wordless*. Only the air thrummed with
the electricity their bodies generated and the soft sound
of the moans that bordered on anguish. As a lover he

was extraordinary, more extraordinary than in all the little fantasies she had kept to herself.

When his mouth found her nipple it set off an avalanche of pleasure. She had to gasp aloud. Excitement was building so rapidly she could hardly remember to breathe. This was the perfect way of blotting out pain and grief. But at such a risk! Her stubborn resistance to him and the power he projected had been her perfect camouflage. Now this headlong surrender. The *enormity* of it. The intense fear and the rapture. Sensation was obscuring everything. Any need for caution. All she was aware of was her overpowering hunger for him. With a few sweeping motions he removed the rest of her clothing. His blue eyes burned at the sight of her body so perfectly designed for a man's loving. They moved over her so intensely he might have been memorising every inch of her, the fine pores of her skin.

Then he was making love to her with such passion yet a curious underlying tenderness that left her dazed with wonder. Both of them had dropped all form of pretence; the masks they had kept in place for so long.

While the rain continued to drum down on the parched earth and the cave was filled with white-hot flashes of intermittent light, the fire that was inside of them burst into a conflagration that finally gave expression to the bewildering pain/pleasure that had plagued them for so long.

This was ecstasy even if they had lost all sense of the morrow.

Another secret.

It was Dana's first waking thought. Around her was silence and the grey pearly light of pre-dawn. As the light brightened the birds would begin to sing in their trillions but for now the silence rang like a hammer on her heart.

Impossible to describe her night. It had been full of fragmentary-coherent dreams and heart-stopping moments when she awoke with a convulsive gasp thinking Logan's hands were caressing her. Her face flushed with colour at the memory and she turned sideways burying her head in the mound of pillows that smelled so beautifully of the native boronia that perfumed the linen press.

Yesterday had been the most traumatic day of her life. It had started so grimly with Jimmy's funeral yet ended in a dazzling ecstasy that redefined life. Two separate momentous experiences. She wasn't a virgin. She and Gerard had shared a warm, caring relationship which she gradually came to understand was not the passionate overwhelming love she really craved. It was she who had broken off the engagement knowing in her heart the right person was out there for both of them. And so it had turned out. Gerard had found his Lucy, but the man who held her under his spell was already in her life. A man who until yesterday had been armoured in discipline, authority, control.

And after the bubble burst and they came back to cold reality?

Neither of them seemed ready to handle what had happened, accepting no amount of mind power could ever wipe it out. For as long as their lovemaking had lasted, both of them had lost all thought of anything but one another. They had breached the iron rule. To keep their physical and psychological distance.

What now?

So deeply was Dana immersed in her thoughts it took a little time for her to register a small voice was calling her name.

Alice.

Dana sprang up from the bed, pulling on her robe as she went.

"Why, darling girl, whatever's the matter?"

Alice stood just outside the door dressed in one of the pretty pin-tucked batiste nighties Dana had bought for her as a balance to the "sensible" apparel Melinda favoured. Her dear plain little face was streaked with tears and her light brown hair free of its plait stuck out in a tangled nimbus around her head. She went straight into Dana's arms, hugging her.

"I went into Mummy's room but she told me to go away. It isn't time to get up. She said she's sick of me and my silly fears. She's not going to look after me anymore."

Shockingly, it was something Melinda said often. Neither Dana nor Jimmy had been able to stop her.

"Mummy doesn't mean it, darling," Dana soothed. "I expect she's still very tired and sad. This is a bad time for all of us."

"It's worse for Daddy." Alice's voice broke on a sob. "Why did he have to die? I'll never forgive him."

Gently Dana drew the child through the door and shut it after her, feeling the grief and frustration that was in the child's small frame.

"It was a terrible accident, Ally. Daddy had no control over what happened to him." Which sadly wasn't strictly true. "He would never have left you. He loved you."

"Then why didn't he stay? Now I'll be more different than ever. I won't have a Daddy."

Dana couldn't answer that. Although she hadn't the slightest doubt Melinda would remarry soon. Melinda had never felt secure on her own. "Hop in with me," Dana invited. "I'll give you a cuddle."

Alice expelled a soft shuddery sigh. "That will be lovely. There was a beastie in my room."

Assorted beasties and bogeymen had long plagued Alice during the hours of darkness. She was a sensitive, imaginative child and, it had to be faced, emotionally disturbed.

"Wasn't your night-light on?" Dana asked, pulling up the covers and settling the little girl against the pillows.

"Mummy doesn't like me to have the night-light, Dana. You know that. She always scolds me. She said it was all your fault filling my head with silly stories."

Dana stroked the fringe from Alice's eyes. "Don't worry, darling, I'll speak to Mummy about it. She doesn't quite realise how much imagination you've got. Lots of children don't like the dark. It's always been part of childhood. A lot of adults don't like it, either. It's nothing to be worried about."

"I like the light on," Alice insisted, already snuggling down. "Dana, do you think I could come to live with you instead of just for a visit?"

Dana tried to cover up her sadness. This was a terrible state of affairs.

"Darling, how could I deprive Mummy of her little girl?"

Alice gave her a very grave adult stare. "She wouldn't miss me. She said she might put me in a boarding school while she travels the world."

This was entirely new to Dana. "When did she say this?"

She got into bed beside Alice while Alice moved into the crook of her shoulder. "Yesterday. She said I was part of the problem with her marriage."

"Oh, rubbish!" Dana couldn't help herself. It just burst out. Melinda depended on her for many things. She would have to flex what little muscle she had for Alice's sake.

"You're really funny when you get mad," Alice giggled. "Daddy said to me once, if I'm not around, find Dana."

"Well, I am your godmother," Dana answered finally.

"And you love me." Alice gave a great sigh of belonging. "Sometimes I really am scared of Mummy. Even the kids at school think she's awful."

Dana pondered on that. "Awful when she's so young and pretty?"

Alice squirmed. "Miss Eldred said, 'It's just awful what she's doing to that child.'"

It was amazing how she caught the teacher's tones. "Surely she wasn't talking about Mummy?"

Alice shot her another look. "Some days when Mummy picks me up she's in a really bad mood."

"Why on earth didn't you tell me?" Dana was appalled.

"You might be so angry at Mummy you might never come to see her and she wouldn't let me see you," Alice answered in her extraordinary way.

"Alice, I would never desert your mother. Or you," Dana said fervently. "You must believe that. Your mother and I have been together since we were little girls. She's almost my sister."

"Then why does she tell you so many lies?"

The skin on Dana's head actually prickled. "Whatever do you mean?"

Alice looked back in genuine puzzlement. "Daddy said she did. Didn't he tell you?"

Dana took her time replying. "Listen, cherub, I hate to say this but too many people have been doing too much talking in front of you. Why don't you curl up now and close your eyes. It's going to be a long, tiring day, I'm afraid. You'll need your sleep."

"Can't I stay awake and listen to the birds? They're so beautiful."

Dana felt a great rush of affection. "The birds will sing for you another day, sweetheart. Get your rest now. We have a lot of travelling to do."

Alice obediently composed herself, giving an exhausted little yawn. "I hope I'll be as beautiful as you are, Dana, when I grow up."

Dana gave the little girl a hug. "Darling, you're going to be a lovely person to be with."

"I want to have a light about me, like you," Alice breathed, her lashes coming down to rest on her cheeks. "Like the picture of an angel."

"That's lovely, darling." Dana was touched.

"Daddy said about the light, but I know exactly what he meant." Alice suddenly opened her eyes and turned her head along the pillow. "Take care of me, Dana?"

"I'll take care of you as long as I live," Dana said staunchly.

"Swear you'll live a long, long time." There was a sudden rush of tears into Alice's big brown eyes.

"You don't have to worry about that." Dana fought to keep her voice steady. "I'm going to live until I'm a hundred and I get a telegram from the Queen."

"Does she really send a telegram?" Alice giggled.

"Yes, she does," Dana said very softly into the little girl's ear.

"Thank you, Dana," Alice answered simply, and almost immediately fell asleep.

Alice was still sleeping when Dana went down to find herself a cup of coffee. The house was quiet, but Mrs. Buchan, the housekeeper, was in the kitchen making preparations for the day.

"So, can I get you a cup of tea, Dana?" she asked as Dana came quietly through the door.

"A cup of coffee would be lovely. Here, let me get it." Dana put a gentle hand on the older woman's shoulder, hearing the uncontrollable tremor of grief in the housekeeper's voice. Mrs. Buchan, in her mid-fifties, had been in the family's employ since she was a girl. Her husband, Manny, Logan's overseer, had started his

working life on the station as a young jackeroo. Both of
them had watched Tyler grow up.

"Toast, dear?" Mrs. Buchan breathed deeply to calm
herself.

"No, I think I'll go for a little walk."

"How about Alice?"

"Don't worry. She'll sleep for a while yet. She woke
up early and came into me."

"You tell me where that little girl would be without
you." Mrs. Buchan shook her head sadly.

Outside in the brilliant early morning sunshine, Dana
walked down the drive, feeling the crunch of gravel beneath her shoes. There wasn't a single cloud in the sky.
It was a deep vivid blue. A sense of foreboding hung
over her, the feeling that life was rushing out of her
control. She had an acute sense, too, of her own sensuality. Not so long ago she thought she had discovered
love with Gerard, but compared to what she had experienced in that explosive storm it now appeared very quiet
and safe. Logan had taught her more about her own body
than she had learned in a lifetime. She had discovered
herself as he had discovered her, unlocking all her
closely held secrets. For that time in the cave there
hadn't been one tiny part of her that hadn't responded
to his touch. Passion at that level was stupendous. It was
also perilous. How, for instance, was she going to live
without it?

CHAPTER FOUR

RESTLESSLY, Dana veered off towards the lake. She could see the exquisite black swans sailing across its glassy green surface with a flotilla of ducks and other waterfowl in attendance. The dense green perimeter of reeds was illuminated by large stands of day lilies, strap-leafed iris and the water-loving arum lilies with their handsome velvety white spathes. It all looked so peaceful, so beautiful, *eternal,* when Jimmy was gone. He had paid a terrible penalty.

She couldn't fathom why he had told his family of a depth of feeling for her, which he had never shown. Of necessity because of their common bond of love and protectiveness for Alice, they had been drawn closely together. Both had tried very hard to shield Alice from a mother who was cold to her.

Trying to find some defence for Melinda, Dana had come to the conclusion Melinda had been emotionally crippled by the early loss of her parents. Dana had once heard her own mother say Melinda was incapable of showing affection. But she was bonded to Dana. Their kinship made Dana unique and Dana had always made allowances for her cousin. They all had. Perhaps in retrospect it had been a mistake. A little toughening up might have made Melinda a more complete person.

Jimmy's death had precipitated a crisis. Alice had lost the loving, caring parent. It was a bruising reality Melinda could and would not show Alice the affection every child needed. Such coldness and Alice's obvious unhappiness troubled every sensitive person who came into their orbit. Dana herself couldn't count the number of times she had felt its chilling effect. Melinda was such a very difficult person. It was because of this Dana had felt compelled to build up a supportive relationship not only for Alice but for Jimmy, who had suffered in his own way. Perhaps her best efforts had complicated things terribly. Without Jimmy to explain his precise emotional attachment, the family might always believe she had deliberately allowed his feelings for her to develop. Truly it looked a hopeless dilemma.

She didn't hear Logan's approach until he was almost up to her, then she turned, her velvety brown eyes almost black with intensity. It came to her with anguish that she wanted him to gather her into his arms, but from the expression on his face, yesterday might never have happened.

"Have you decided what you're going to do?" he asked tautly.

Even the set of his body had a daunting authority. She looked away across the lake, her heart beating painfully. "If I could stay, Logan, I would."

"So what's so damned important to take you off?"

They were caught in the old minefield of antagonism. "I have a career. A successful career, but I don't have a fortune behind me. Not like you."

"I'll take care of that," he said curtly.

"I know you would, but nothing could persuade me to take money from you, Logan."

"Dana, please." He took hold of her shoulders, turned her to him. "Ainslie is desperately in need of comfort. Sandra, too. You can help."

"I know that." Dana's eyes filled with tears. "And I'm so terribly sad. Please don't be angry with me, Logan. I'm so upset myself, I feel I want someone to take care of *me*."

"I'll take care of you until the cows come home," he

clipped off. "God, Dana, if I let you, you'd have me eating out of your hands."

Incredulously she heard his words, assimilating them through every cell of her body. "But you can't handle that?" she questioned. What was power without love?

His brilliant gaze was the distillation of his passionate nature. "You're running, too, Dana," he told her bluntly. "Hell, you can't wait to get away. But neither of us is going to forget what happened."

"Knowing you, Logan, you'll give it your best shot." She couldn't prevent the upsurge of bitterness.

He let out a sigh that seemed filled with terrible doubts. "It's going to be a long time before I can part you in my mind from Tyler."

"You've just got to be Number One," she said in a low, weary tone.

"So what are you telling me?" he challenged her fiercely.

"I'm telling you *nothing*. You've already decided what you want to believe."

Her eyes were so dark, so beautiful, they could hide many secrets. He wanted desperately to know them all.

She half turned as her voice broke, hair and skin gleaming in the vivid shimmering light. She could taste the pain it was so intense.

"Dana." He came after her immediately, catching hold of her bare arm. "I'm sorry. God, I'm sorry. I don't even know what I'm saying. We're all hurting. I'm only asking you to use your gift."

"Gift, what gift?" She wasn't comforted by his touch. She was on fire. Both of them were still on the thin edge of control.

"People want to talk to you, Dana," he said, his eyes searching her face. "They want to confide in you. I suppose it's called healing."

"But it's Alice who's most in need of me now."

"And how are any of us going to find a way around Melinda? No court will take a child off its mother unless the charges are very serious. Melinda may be damned awful to Alice, but it's emotional abuse and it's mostly hidden. How the hell did you have such a ghastly cousin anyway?"

Dana didn't allow herself to consider she had asked herself the same question. "You've always been rough on her," she accused him.

"I agree." His tone was unapologetic. "I don't seem capable of hiding my dislike. Melinda wrecked my brother's life. She tried to wreck this family. She's turning my little niece into a real mess. Frankly, I find that very hard to stomach. What's more, I'm sick to death of listening to you defend her."

"And I'm sick of listening to you." Dana stopped abruptly, afraid she was about to crumble.

"Then isn't it hell for us to want one another so badly?" he retaliated. "I couldn't bear the thought of you out of my life, yet I don't know how to reach you. You're very valuable to us, Dana. We just can't do without you."

"Valuable? I don't deserve that." His words stirred her so much, her heart pounded in her chest. He was alternatively sharp then seductive. No wonder she was in such a state of constant emotional flux. "I know I'm the intermediary between Melinda and the family."

His expression softened. "Alice is in trouble, Dana. You know that, don't you?"

"Of course I do." She bit her lip.

"I can't walk softly around Melinda. Alice is my brother's child, my niece, a Dangerfield. I'm going to make sure she has a good life."

"And I'm going to help you, Logan," Dana responded with fervour. "I promise you I'll have a serious talk with Melinda."

He groaned, his eyes fierce. "I've heard all about your serious talks. I know how much you love Alice, how much she loves you, but in the end all the talk turns out to be a monologue. When has Melinda ever *listened?*"

It was true. "So *you* talk to her." Dana's voice rose. "You're all powerful."

"I intend to," he said decisively. "Melinda will be financially secure for the rest of her life, but she's not getting what she may have counted on. I've seen to that."

"How?" Dana was completely thrown off stride.

"I had a damned good talk to Tyler last time he was home," Logan told her tersely. "As a family we haven't been wasting our time all these years. We've worked hard to hold on to all we've got. The bulk of the money will be held in trust for Alice. I administer that trust, as you know."

"So there's a new will?"

"There is, my lady. I don't mind your knowing. If Melinda is smart, she'll accept it. It will advantage her nothing going out on the attack. I should tell you, too, so you won't get too emotional. Tyler left a legacy to you."

The shock of it almost sent her reeling. *"No."*

"You didn't know about it?" He smiled tightly, like a tiger.

Her face flamed and she was sorely tempted to hit him. "God, Logan, I hate you."

His handsome mouth twitched in bleak humour. "Sometimes that's the way I feel about you. It's rather a lot of money," he added.

"I don't want it." Her turbulent emotions matched his exactly.

"Maybe you could even quit work," he suggested.

"Go on. Have your hateful fun," she cried.

"It would be the only fun I could have at a time like

this," he pointed out grimly. "I don't think Melinda is going to like it."

"Melinda can think what she damned well likes." Dana was so angry she fairly trembled. "She does anyway. I don't want to say this, but she lies."

"No kidding."

"Why are we fighting, Logan?" she asked bleakly.

"It seemed like the best solution up until now." It sounded unbearably cynical but at that moment he wanted her so badly he clenched his fists until his knuckles whitened. His brother's death was a terrible tragedy and Dana was his good and beautiful friend.

At the look in his eyes, the half-expected rejection, something seemed to die in her. "I'm going back to the house, Logan," she said.

"That's just what I'm doing," he said.

"Then why don't you take another route?" Her voice was cold and dismissive.

He reached for her, holding her still without any physical effort. "Are you telling me what I can do on my own land?"

She tried to pull away. "I sure am. You're like one of those feudal barons, aren't you?"

"Not that I'm aware," he said coolly, but his blue eyes burned.

"Oh, yes, the whole persona fits you perfectly, just like a second skin."

"Then surely I can demand anything of any beautiful woman who passes my way?" he suggested with the powerful urge to fold her in his arms.

"It's part of it, yes," she hit back.

"Like yesterday?" He was so angry, for a moment his grip tightened painfully.

"I suppose now you think you can have me anytime you want." She was shocked at herself but determined to say it.

"Leave it there, Dana," he warned, his eyes fixed on her.

"It may be years before I have another opportunity," she retorted in bitter irony.

"All right, then." Like yesterday, his strong will fled him, leaving only the desperate hunger he believed nothing else could fill. He swept her into his arms, silencing her lovely mouth with a kiss that was without a skerrick of tenderness, holding the kiss powerfully until her furious resistance yielded in sheer surrender and her own needs were utterly betrayed. When he released her, her face was flaming and her dark eyes sheened with tears.

"You brute!" When she had let herself fall fathoms into that kiss.

"Tell me something I don't know," he said with a kind of self-contempt. "I've always wanted to make love to you, Dana. Didn't you know? Stretching right back to the day when you simply burst into my life like some exotic flower."

Want? What was want when she needed so much more from him? "Nevertheless you made sure you kept me at a great distance."

"I know I *attempted* to." His voice was suddenly wry.

"And succeeded rather well. You even got yourself engaged to Phillipa."

"And I'm very fond of her, but it wasn't the classic love at first sight. Maybe it even had something to do with the fact you were marrying your...Jeremy, wasn't it?"

"Gerard, as you very well know." A sudden wind tore at her hair skeined out around her face, causing her to turn away.

"So both of us made a mistake."

"I like that, Logan. You making a mistake," she said in response.

"I don't mean to make another."

She had begun walking, now she turned on her heel. "Does that hold some message for me?" she asked, her face lit by pride.

"You're welcome to see one in it if you like."

She made a sound of distress and shook her head. "We can never be together five minutes without this happening."

It was perfectly true, and under the truth a very good reason. He closed the short space between them. "And I apologise. Most of it is my fault. But it's just as I told you, I have warring feelings about you, Dana."

"It's damned hard to live with," she said bitterly.

"For you and for me." He caught her hand, raised it to his mouth in one of his totally disconcerting gestures. "I didn't want to upset you. I want you to stay."

"As Alice's comforter, or your mistress?" she asked, unable to resist it, but dazed at the thought.

"Well...both."

Some note in his voice made her look up at him sharply, only to find him smiling at her, that rare, charm-the-birds-out-of-the-trees smile that so illuminated his dark face.

"You're insufferable." She was losing the battle to fight his strong aura.

"I know." He tipped up her chin, kissed her briefly but with a haunting sympathy that stayed with her for the rest of the day.

The will reading went badly. Melinda sat white-faced with bitter resentment as Logan read through the four page document, mute until the moment when Logan announced in dispassionate tones Dana's legacy. Then hell broke loose. Melinda rose so swiftly from her chair that if it hadn't been for its substantial weight she would have sent it flying. As it was, her leather armchair rolled back on its casters, scraping the parquet around the Persian rug.

"I don't believe this." For the first time Melinda showed the anger and hostility she usually kept so carefully under wraps.

"All of us are aware Tyler thought very highly of Dana," Logan said, his handsome face without expression.

"Felt highly of her! Is that what it was?" Melinda was totally unable to accept she was not the main beneficiary let alone Dana had been left a considerable sum of money.

"Please sit down, Melinda," Dana begged. "I won't, of course, be accepting it."

"Of course you *will*," Logan cast her a brief glance. "Tyler counted on you for a great deal."

"He was in love with her!" Inexplicably Melinda laughed as if at a joke. "He revelled in her company, the warmth he wouldn't let me give him. I never counted on my own cousin ruining my marriage."

While Dana drew a sharp breath preparatory to answering, Ainslie burst in. "I think you took care of that yourself, Melinda."

"I did not!" Melinda was too far gone to care. "She was always around us. I can still hear their laughter in my ears. Do you think I'd speak like this if it weren't true?"

"Yes," Dana answered without hesitation. "I've always supported you, Melinda, but I'm not prepared to let you destroy my good name. Stop this unforgivable offence right now. I want to be cleared fully. Jimmy—" She corrected herself immediately. "*Tyler* and I were friends. Our common bond was Alice."

"Before God it's true," Melinda announced ringingly. "I even caught you one time."

A deep unstoppable anger took hold of Dana. She felt

she could protest her innocence forever and never be believed. She shot out of her chair like an avenging angel, grasping her cousin's upper arms tightly. "You'll never drag me down, Melly," she promised. "I'll never understand why you want to."

"If you hadn't been around he would have come back to me," Melinda exclaimed with a high moral tone.

"Well, you had to make sure we all knew," Logan said in a harsh voice. "Now that you've got that off your chest, would you mind resuming your seat, Melinda? There's more to get through. Despite your disappointment I'm sure you're going to be very comfortable with five million. Tyler's main concern was for Alice."

"I can't see why she needs all that money when she has you to look after her," Melinda retorted, her pale blue eyes almost colourless with anger. "I know I can fight this."

"I would advise you not to," Logan looked at her for a space of time. "I want it on record we'll continue to exercise our rights as Alice's family. We'll want to see her and have a say in her education."

"Please, Melinda," Ainslie implored as Melinda's expression slid into one of regained bargaining power. "We must all co-operate for Alice's sake. My little granddaughter is all that is left to me of Tyler. I did love him so."

"He wasn't the husband I imagined he was going to be," Melinda continued in the flat ugly tone she had always kept from the family. "As for your rights with Alice? Well, we'll see. I'm not dependent on you Dangerfields anymore. You never wanted me from day one when you were always so affable to Dana. You should have thrown her out."

"For having a heart, Melinda?" Logan challenged, and his voice reverberated around the room. "Her loving manner with Alice alone would have endeared her to us. You're so anxious to belittle your cousin when she has always been so loyal to you. Why *is* that?''

''She betrayed me.'' Melinda's voice cracked with emotion. ''She took everything I ever wanted.''

''No, Melly.'' Dana let out a long, terrible sigh, at that moment she could have killed Melinda for the lie. ''It was always the other way about. Everything was given to *you*. We all did it. It was a way of compensating for what you'd suffered.''

''Well, you don't have to worry about me now,'' Melinda said in a strange singsong voice. ''I've got enough money to live my own life. I bet you're happy with your little sum. You must have planned it all along.''

There was total silence in the room, then Logan rose from behind the massive mahogany desk with detached disgust. ''Our business is concluded here. Your plane is due in just over thirty minutes, Melinda. I'll drive you down to the airstrip. I'd like to say goodbye to Alice there. May I wish you a safe journey. This has been a terrible time for all of us. I know none of us wants to compound the grief with disharmony in the family. We want the very best for Alice.''

Outside in the hallway, Melinda stalked up the central staircase the very picture of outrage, while Ainslie, looking paper white and suddenly frail, clutched at Dana's arm.

''Surely you can't go back with her now, dear?''

Dana was almost at the point of abandoning her commitments but she couldn't. ''I must, Ainslie,'' she said regretfully. ''I know Melinda. She says many things she doesn't mean. She really needs me. Alice, too.''

Ainslie's expression went wry. ''It's wonderful you can feel for your cousin like you do. Today she was absolutely ghastly.''

"I apologise for her," Dana said. "I think you should be in your bed. You're in shock. When is Sandra due home?"

"Shortly. Jack is bringing her." Ainslie sighed heavily. "If we hadn't lost Tyler I think they were coming around to announcing their engagement. They've always been very happy in one another's company."

"Yes," Dana murmured. "Here, let me take you upstairs." She slipped an arm around Ainslie's waist, leading the older woman towards the stairs. "I have a number of commitments I must honour, but can't you come to me for a little while. A change of scene. I don't have a mansion but I do have a very comfortable guest room. We could talk and I could bring Alice to see you. Melinda won't mind. Sandra could come, too, if she liked. We could manage."

For the first time Ainslie smiled. "You're very kind, Dana. One can see it in those great dark eyes. I'm tottering today but I just might take you up on your offer. I need solace a million more times now."

Upstairs Dana knocked on Melinda's door then opened it without waiting for an answer. Melinda was standing in the centre of the room vigorously brushing her short blond hair away from her face.

"God, Melly, you must want to hurt me badly to have said all that. What gets into you?"

"Nobody puts any value on me," Melinda explained in a shaking voice. "Sometimes I find the way everyone loves you utterly insupportable. If I had to be born again it would be as *you*. Even my own daughter doesn't love me like she loves you." Melinda threw down the brush and collapsed into a chair. "I'm going to find someone who really cares about me."

"I understand how you feel, Melly," Dana said, wishing her cousin had just a little more iron in her soul. "But you have to learn how to *give*."

Suddenly Melinda's face changed. "Be mad at me, Dana," she said. "You have a right."

Dana sighed. "Be mad at me" had always been her cousin's way of showing shame or remorse. "I'll go and get Alice ready. I'm all packed. Put your luggage at the door. One of the men will take care of it."

At the airstrip with the charter plane waiting to take them to the nearest domestic terminal, Alice, high in Logan's arms, threw her arms around his neck, burrowing into it, crying with the pain of departure.

"Please, Uncle Logan, don't forget me."

"Miss Dangerfield," he said in a mock-stern voice, "would you mind repeating that?" He lifted her chin so that Alice staring into his eyes saw only love and a devotion that would last a lifetime. Her uncle Logan represented safety and comfort. He was so tall and strong and though he didn't look like Daddy, his voice it suddenly occurred to her was like Daddy's only darker or deeper and more definite somehow. "You could have me back for the holidays," she ventured.

"We could indeed." Logan kissed her cheek lightly then set her down, resting his hand on the top of her head. Alice was wearing a yellow dress that gave off a bright glow, but her smile was small and sad. "Be a good girl, sweetheart. Grandma might be coming to Sydney to stay with Dana for a while so you have that to look forward to, then the Christmas holidays. We'll fix something up with Mummy."

Instantly Alice's cheeks took on a little bloom.

"Goodbye, then, Logan," Melinda said stiffly. "I don't imagine I would be included in the invitation. I've had no refuge here."

"That was one of your choices, Melinda," Logan answered in quiet somewhat weary tones.

Melinda grabbed for Alice's hand and began to walk

towards the waiting Cessna, leaving Dana to say her goodbyes.

"It doesn't exactly sound good," Logan murmured ruefully.

"I'll speak to her, Logan," Dana promised. "Things will work out."

"Is that the prognosis for us?" His eyes were jewels; his words so disturbing she put a hand that suddenly trembled to her breast. "*Is* there an us?" She felt the fire run through her, the tremendous swell of desire. Just to stand near was like being trapped in a magnetic field.

"You're very bright, Dana. Very intelligent. There always was an us and always some reason for hiding it. When Ainslie wants to come to you, I'll fly her in. You might find some time for me. In the meantime so you won't find it quite so easy to block me from your mind..."

As his voice trailed off he took her by the shoulders. The next moment she felt his mouth close over hers, its sensuous contours warm, alive, her soft face revelling in the slight rasp of his shaved skin. He kissed her, not gently but matching perfectly the emotion of the moment so her lips yielded beneath his, every inch of her body sensitized and sheened with excitement. Griefs ebbed away as the kiss lengthened, searing her in golden heat.

Logan's brand, she thought. She would never be free of it. At the same time it gave her great energy and the strength to go on.

CHAPTER FIVE

THE next couple of weeks were a mixed bag so far as Dana was concerned. On the one hand she was thrilled and delighted to win a prestigious award for excellence in Children's Portrait Photography, further enhancing her career; on the other, trying to be there for Melinda and Alice proved harrowing.

The loss of one's husband is an enormous crisis in a woman's life and although the marriage had not been a happy one with neither partner making the right moves to improve it, Melinda had fallen into a depression that involved either venting her feelings very forcibly or bouts of sobbing that bordered on hysteria.

Alice, suffering in her own way, had gone back to school, but it was Dana in the main who collected her after school or when Alice's own tantrums became too overwhelming for her teacher and fellow pupils to cope with. The fact Alice's behaviour had been tolerated so long was due to her attendance at a small private school where the teachers had the necessary time to try and establish a good relationship with her and help her over an extremely difficult period in her young life. A school psychologist had even been called in to observe Alice but when Alice had refused in no uncertain terms to have her near, the young woman had thrown up her hands in defeat. Alice's main temper tantrums occurred when the teachers tried to get her to do something she didn't want, as in group activities or when it was time to go home, unless Dana was to collect her. Finally when everyone had done their best and the other parents were beginning to voice their complaints, the headmistress requested an interview with Melinda.

"I'm not going," Melinda told Dana flatly.

"Melly, you'll have to." Dana sat with her arm around Alice's shivering frame. Almost a half hour had gone by since Dana had arrived home with Alice in tow. Alice had pushed another little girl so hard the child had fallen back against a desk and sustained a bruise to the temple. Not only that, the child's grandmother was on the board of trustees. Melinda hadn't answered her phone, so the school had rung Dana who at this stage was well known to them.

"I don't have to do anything," Melinda said, oblivious to Dana's ongoing hassles. "There's something wrong with Alice. It has to be in the Dangerfield's history. There's absolutely nothing wrong with me. When did I ever give trouble at school?"

"Quite often as I recall," Dana pointed out dryly. Melinda right through primary and secondary school had been a controversial little person with a habit of fabricating stories. A kind of payback to classmates out of favour.

"I hardly expect you to stick up for me," Melinda said bitterly. "Everyone seems to think so highly of you, *you* front up to Mrs. Forster. I'm in no condition to sit through interviews."

Mrs. Forster, a handsome woman in her early fifties, received Dana very graciously, listening quietly while Dana explained why Melinda was unable to attend the interview.

"I understand completely." Mrs. Forster's shrewd grey eyes were fixed sympathetically on Dana's face. "We were all shocked by the tragedy. It explains so much of Alice's behaviour. On the other hand..."

For the next twenty minutes Dana sat patiently

through a stream of constant concerns. Alice was highly intelligent but did her level best to hide it. On her good days she was very endearing. She was good with little Samantha Richards, for instance. Samantha had a mild form of cerebral palsy. Alice's gentle kindness at least was judged admirable. But with the others... Here Mrs. Forster threw up her hands. Alice's behaviour was very uneven. She was either aggressive or withdrawn. She wanted to sit in a corner and read books all day, telling everyone to keep away, including her teacher.

Finally it was suggested it might be better for Alice to take time off school while she tried to cope with her obvious unhappiness.

Against Melinda's strenuous protest the school was shirking its responsibilities, Alice had her enforced holiday with Dana, taking her goddaughter at the weekend. To "give me a break," Melinda's own words. It curtailed Dana's social life but she wasn't concerned. Alice was very important to her and in great need of emotional support. How it was all going to end, however, she didn't know.

Ainslie's visit considerably eased the burden. In her grief Ainslie found great comfort in the very nearness of her little granddaughter. Because it suited her, Melinda had offered no objection beyond the mandatory bitter comments to Alice's staying over, and Alice, for her part, sensitive, intelligent little girl that she was, realised her being there was very important to her grandmother. Alice, the school rebel with a history of causing trouble, was markedly different when it came to "hurt people." Just as she took special care with her little friend, Samantha, at school, Alice showed the utmost concern for her grandmother's well-being.

To Dana's mind they moved closer every day, taking walks in the park together, sharing an ice cream, visiting the beach and going for drives. In this way Dana was free to keep up with most of her commitments although she curtailed her hours so she could be home for Ainslie and Alice. Despite Ainslie's obvious delight in her granddaughter, Dana realised it was tiring for Ainslie to keep going when she was physically and mentally laid low. Still, by the time the fortnight was over Ainslie was showing a heartening recovery.

"I feel exactly the same as you, Granny," Alice told her gently, putting a comforting arm around her grandmother. "We're sad for Daddy, but us two can stick together."

"Yes, darling, we can," Ainslie replied, smiling through her tears. "*Us two*. That is as it should be. Us two from now on."

Logan couldn't accompany Ainslie to Sydney for her stay. Pressure of business had allowed him only enough time to fly her to the nearest domestic airport. Mara was going in for organic beef in a big way and there were many meetings and discussions about this, but Logan had rung to say his schedule was fine for picking Ainslie up for the return flight. Ainslie even suggested she might be able to take Alice back with her, but here Melinda put her foot down.

"I can't begin to contemplate it," she told Dana. "Too far away. And Ainslie knows it. No, Dana, don't bother trying to win me over," she warned, catching sight of Dana's expression. "Alice stays. I have you to help me and I don't want to lose control to the Dangerfields. To hell with them all!"

Dana felt a mounting excitement not unmixed with trepidation as the morning of Logan's arrival approached. Much as some elements in their relationship disturbed her, by the Friday afternoon she felt like a bonfire blazing away merrily.

"You won't find it so easy to block me from your

mind,'' Logan had said. Easy? It had proved impossible.
She still heard his voice in her head, still trembled at his
remembered touch. She thought she had had a good idea
of what it was like to be in love. She had been a little
bit in love with all her boyfriends since she had started
dating. She thought she had loved Gerard, had become
engaged to him, but nothing had prepared her for the
enormous heart-stopping pleasure she took in Logan. It
was infinitely greater than any pleasure she had ever
known. Pleasure, a certain apprehension, the melting
heat of excitement. She couldn't wait for him to arrive.
The anticipatory glow almost made up for the grinding
disappointment she had experienced when he had been
unable to accompany Ainslie on her arrival.

She arrived home a little later than she had hoped
Friday afternoon, apologising to Ainslie who met her at
the front door.

"Darling girl, come in and relax," Ainslie said, drawing her in. "You're much too pressured. I feel a lot of
it is due to me."

"Not at all. I love having you here." Dana deposited
her things on a chair. "Where's Alice?" she asked.

"She's changing her shoes for joggers." Ainslie
laughed, her cheeks pink. "We're going for a walk in
the park. She just loves the fountain, the way the sun
makes those little rainbows in the spray."

"Excellent! I can have my shower." Dana slipped out
of her linen jacket. "It's been one long hot day. A
shower will feel fantastic. What say we have a nice family dinner at Ecco." She referred to one of the small
superb restaurants in the area, specialising in Italian food
as the name would imply. Alice adored "Italian."

"Lovely." Ainslie stretched out a hand to pat Dana's
soft cheek. "Logan will be here tomorrow, but I want
to tell you now how much I've appreciated being here
this fortnight, Dana. I've loved having your company,

enjoying little Alice. It's not a feeling of visiting. It's a feeling of being *home*."

Standing outside the door of Dana's apartment, Logan hesitated for a moment thinking up an excuse for why he hadn't let them know he was arriving a day early. Alice enjoyed surprises? Ainslie would greet him as she always did with arms out-thrown. But Dana? He had to confront the fact he had arrived early because he felt maddened to see her. It all came of making love to her. The unbearable involuntary longing. This from a man who had prided himself on his self-sufficiency, his content with his own company. No more. The longing came as a severe jolt. Every day it seemed to get worse. He could hear music coming from inside. A violin. Not classical. Something modern, elegant, distinctive. Probably Nigel Kennedy, he guessed. He pressed the buzzer, gave it a few moments, suddenly aware of a charge of adrenaline. What exactly would happen if Dana came to the door? Would he suddenly grab her? Draw her into an impassioned embrace? Hell, he felt wild enough.

But no one came. The music played on.

Exploratively he put his hand on the doorknob expecting to encounter resistance from the lock, only the knob turned. That was decidedly odd.

He stepped inside, feeling a surge of anxiety. The apartment looked wonderful. Like Dana. The combination of colours of fabrics, of ornamentation, the beautiful flowers.

"Dana?" he called, his tone urgent. "Anyone at home?" Surely in this day and age when security was paramount, she would think to lock her front door.

Beyond the seductively haunting sound of the violin another sound reached his ears. Running water. Someone was home. Maybe Ainslie. Dana and Alice could be out.

It was getting on for late afternoon even if the sun was full of blazing sparkle.

"Hello?" He moved farther into the apartment, experiencing a tightening anxiety until someone appeared. He moved past the empty guest bedroom, the sliding-glass door open to the balcony incandescent with massed pink and white daisies in blue-glazed pots.

He found her in the master bedroom, or rather in the shower of the ensuite, eyes closed, head tilted back as the water ran in rivers over her exquisite woman's body. He knew he had to, but he couldn't. He could not look away. His very breath caught in his throat. She was creamy pale to her toes. Swan's throat, delicate shoulders, a tilt to her breasts with their pointed rose nipples, the long curve of her back, the small perfectly shaped buttocks, the slender straight legs. He wished he could draw. He wished he was a gifted painter who could seize the moment, capture it on canvas, so he could look at it forever. But then she reached forward, making an effort with her eyes closed to turn off the faucets. Only a few moments, yet it had been timeless delight. But not for the world would he embarrass her. He moved back soundlessly, deciding the best thing he could do was start all over again.

The doorbell. Dana heard it just as she reached for a towel. Surely they weren't back already? These little walks usually spun out to an hour. Perhaps it was too hot. Hastily she put on her robe, careless of the fact her wet body was leaving sprinkles of damp all over the short pink satin gown. Walking back through the hallway, she shook her long hair free of its coil, feeling its bulk and softness against her nape.

The door wasn't locked, causing her a frisson of anxiety. She hadn't thought to check it after Ainslie and Alice had left, which was a mistake. Usually Ainslie

snibbed the lock and pulled the door after her. Better to
say nothing however.

"You're early..." she cried, sweeping the door open
to confront them. Instead of Ainslie and Alice, Logan
was staring down at her with open fascination, his gaze
so deep she thought she could drown in that radiant blue-
ness.

"You're right. By a day. And you look so...
delectable." In fact she held him utterly. He could smell
the perfume of whatever she had used in the shower.
Gardenia? The sweet freshness of her skin. Beads of
moisture like dewdrops ran from the base of her throat
down the shadowed valley between the lapels of her
robe. For a moment he thought he would bend his head
and tongue up those drops. He badly wanted to. He even
stepped forward, his features tautening.

"Welcome," Dana breathed. Her blood was racing as
the sensuality that was in him communicated itself powerfully to her. This complex intimacy. She had never
known anything like it.

"No kiss for me?" he mocked, desperate now for the
taste of her mouth.

"Maybe a gentle one." She stood on tiptoe, shut her
eyes and presented her mouth, every pulse throbbing,
every nerve tingling and alive.

Just to touch her was to realise the depth of his hunger. He gathered her close to him with one arm, amused
yet on fire with the way she had jokingly made her full
rounded mouth even more pouty. Her body against his.
Her beautiful naked body beneath the soft satin robe. A
gentle one? Hell, he wasn't a boy. He was a man racked
with hunger.

The kiss lasted a long time as their defences unfurled
and fell away.

"God, I've missed you," he groaned, his hands cruis-
ing with controlled yearning over her body. This wasn't

the time to act on his feelings. He was already living dangerously. He'd totally flipped his cool over this one, velvet-eyed woman.

"I've missed you, too," she murmured, seduced at every level.

"You can't invite me into your bedroom, I suppose?" To kiss her was to want it all.

"No," she said regretfully, her body alight.

"Damn!" He tried to joke, even gave a little laugh, when he was thoroughly aroused. "You're obviously not as reckless as I am." And what a glorious risk! He bent his head, kissed her again, feeling with a hard jolt of pleasure the tip of her tongue mating with his.

"Ainslie and Alice will be home soon," she warned him shakily, trying to fight down her own tempestuous sensations. "They've only gone for a walk."

"Hell, when I want you so very very much." Another kiss. This time a little rough. He let his hand skim her back, feeling the slick satin warmth from her body. He urged her closer, closer so he could feel her breasts crushed against him, the thud of her heart.

"Logan!" There was a little flutter of panic in her soft cry. Panic and acknowledged desire to surrender.

"You're right to be scared," he rasped, moving her hair away from her ear so he could nibble the succulent lobe. "I could kiss you until hell freezes over."

"And it's fabulous." She had to swallow hard on all the emotion that was in her. "But I should get dressed." Any moment Ainslie and Alice could return.

His eyes were electric. "I think *no* clothes work better," he drawled. "Oh, all right." He relented, dropping his hands before he arrived at a point neither of them could handle. "Go, then. Put on something pretty, though you look great in anything. I've a mind to take us all to dinner."

*   *   *

Melinda chose the following morning to pay a courtesy call. A gesture so phony, Dana was disgusted.

"Just so they don't decide to whisk Alice away," she mouthed at Dana the moment she stepped in the front door.

As soon as Alice saw her mother, her voice quavered and she looked like she was about to cry. "Hello, Mummy," she said anxiously.

"Hello, Alice." Melinda barely looked at her daughter. She walked to the hall mirror and fluffed up her hair. "Logan arrived yet? A lot of traffic from the Hilton." She continued to study her makeup intently.

The seemingly offhand remark had the crack of a whip. "How did you know he was staying at the Hilton?" Dana stared at the cousin she knew so well. And didn't know at all.

"I'm not dumb." Melinda glanced away from her reflection. "He usually stays there, doesn't he?"

"But he wasn't supposed to arrive until this morning. I told you that on the phone."

"I know." Melinda shrugged carelessly. "But it just so happens a friend saw you all dining out last night and passed it on. Silly to think I might have been invited. Anyway, I gave Logan a call just before I popped over."

Dismay caused Dana to react forcibly. "Whatever for?" Once Melinda started talking to Logan everything went wrong.

Patches of red stood out on Melinda's cheekbones, the only indication she was flurried. "Don't be difficult, Dee. Just keeping in touch. I would like you to remember I'm the Dangerfield around here."

"That's funny. I thought you'd forgotten it entirely," Dana retaliated, sickness stirring.

"How you love to have your little digs," Melinda responded with venom. "You don't have what it takes to land a Dangerfield. No way. Logan has a dark side to him.''

"You and he both," Dana burst out feelingly. "You didn't make any trouble for me, did you?''

Melinda's blue eyes were wide and guileless. "Good heavens, no. All I did was say hello. I wish you all the good things in life a million times over." She smiled at Dana as she said it, but Dana was unhappily aware of the jaggedness that was in her. Melinda, she had come to realise, revelled in sowing the seeds of discord. It was almost a sport to her. She had also developed a compulsion to destroy the blossoming relationship between Dana and Logan.

Dana was sure of it the minute Logan arrived. One glance at his hard handsome face revealed the difference. One exchanged greeting. The formality was back in place. The ease and warmth of the previous evening had just as suddenly been reversed. They were back to their familiar *distance*. Only Ainslie's gentle presence as Dana drove them to the light aircraft terminal saved the situation. The constraints were on. Dana was positive now it had something to do with Melinda.

Melinda, of course, denied it. "Would I do anything to upset you when I desperately need your help?" She had rounded on Dana as she and Alice left to go home.

"I'm sure you would," Dana had replied, feeling defeated and betrayed. Melinda shifted moods so often she might have suffered from multiple personalities.

With Ainslie and Logan safely back on Mara, things continued as before. Alice came to Dana at the weekend, unchallenged because Dana simply couldn't bear to let the little girl languish. Something had to bring it to a head, but not in a way Dana had ever contemplated. One Sunday evening when Dana returned Alice to her mother's care they found the house was empty and a letter addressed to Dana in Melinda's handwriting propped up on the mantelpiece. Childlike, Alice was intrigued more than worried. She ran through the house, room after room, checking her mother wasn't simply hiding. Her mother's behaviour was often strange. Meanwhile Dana read through the letter thinking she would never forget the contents.

Melinda had gone away to find herself. She had in fact taken a Qantas flight to London that very day. She made it sound like a harmless joy flight. Obviously she had been planning the whole operation for some time, Dana thought dazedly. Melinda intended to travel the world. She was going to stay in the best hotels, treat herself to some really beautiful clothes. Furthermore she intended to marry just as soon as she found the right man. A man who would cherish her and appreciate all she had to offer. She stressed she needed her freedom. She could not be "shackled with a child." Alice was in good hands. As an heiress she had a secure future.

And to hell with the emotional well-being! Dana leaned back in her chair momentarily staring sightlessly at the ceiling.

"I'm going to get out from under your shadow, Dana," Melinda concluded. "And about time, too. Life has been so damned disappointing. Never what I hoped for. Maybe things would have been different if my mother and father had lived. Anyway now I've got sole control of the money, I'm going to make my dreams come true. Bright and beautiful as you are, you'll never land that lord of all creation, Logan. He'll never forgive or forget the role you played in Jimmy's life. Logan's woman would have to be *perfect*. And he has already decided you're not."

With your help, Melly, Dana thought bleakly, afraid now to contact him.

But despite the pressure of her work, the difficulties

of adjustment, despite *everything,* Dana was able to manage. What held her and Alice together was the love they had for each other. On some occasions Dana was able to take Alice along on location, other times she was forced to employ an agency nanny. That was the worst part. Dana ran herself ragged but whenever she arrived home it was to Alice begging her never to leave her again. Much as the kind and competent nanny tried to soothe and please, Alice remained intractable. Eventually Dana had to face the truth. She couldn't cope on her own. Someone had to be on hand full-time to combat Alice's profound sense of loss and abandonment. Alice needed her family around her. She had taken overlong to work up the courage to contact Logan and Ainslie. The reason being her sensed estrangement from Logan the day they had parted. Now the moment had arrived. She could put it off no longer.

"How do you feel about going to visit Grandma and Uncle Logan?" Dana asked one evening, watching Alice put a quite difficult jigsaw puzzle Dana had just bought her together.

Alice who had been hunched over her project sat up straight, a beaming smile on her face. "Oh, that would be lovely! I adore it on Mara. You'll have to come, too."

Dana confronted the issue head-on. "I'll have to stay here, Alice, while I get an important project under way. I have a solo showing early December."

"But after that?" Alice began to look less happy.

"If it's all right with Uncle Logan I'll come later," Dana said, anxious not to disappoint her.

That settled it for Alice. "Uncle Logan will be all for it." She grinned. "Let's go to Mara. It'll be fun."

Dana should have acted there and then but decided to wait until the next day when Alice wasn't around to put through a call. It would be agonising to have to explain Melinda's defection and not in front of the child.

Morning, like most mornings, proved hectic. She was out of the studio for most of the time on a fashion shoot checking in with Becky her seventeen-year-old assistant and apprentice who fielded all her calls. Dana had first seen Becky on a T.V. programme about youth unemployment and felt constrained to offer a job to the tough, valiant little Becky who wanted "to make something of herself." A snap decision that had worked very happily.

"You've had a visitor," Becky told her on the last call-in. "Best-lookin' guy I've ever seen. Tall, dark and handsome with brilliant blue eyes. High flyer. *Very.* Moves in all the best circles, I'd say."

"He didn't leave a name?" As if he *had* to with that excellent description of Logan.

"And he gave me such a smile," Becky crowed. "Said he'd be back. I told him you'd be free for lunch. You're such a terrific compassionate person you're not gettin' to enjoy yourself."

Nerves on edge, Dana took a taxi, thankful she was wearing a favourite sand-coloured Armani suit, an expensive badge of confidence. On a lot of assignments she opted for casual clothes but this had been a high-fashion shoot, something of an occasion. The clothes had been wonderful, especially a red lace evening dress she took quite a fancy to. Christmas was coming up. Lots of parties she realised she wouldn't be attending. Alice was her first priority.

When she arrived back at the studio it was to find Logan looking the picture of cool, hard elegance, wearing a beautiful city suit, his enviable hair gleaming blue-black, shorter, the deep wave controlled with excellent barbering.

"Haven't you led me a merry dance?" he drawled, lifting himself out of one of the leather armchairs and rising to his impressive six-three.

"For once in my life I was hoping you wouldn't hurry

up." Becky grinned cheekily. "Logan has been telling me the most marvellous stories about life in the Outback." Too young to hide her enthrallment, Becky's pert, animated little face glowed.

"I'm pleased." Dana inclined her cheek as Logan barely brushed it with his lips. "This is such a surprise, Logan," she said in a poised voice when the familiar charge of electricity was kicking in. "Are you in town on business?"

"One all-important appointment late afternoon," he told her. "It's been set up for some time, otherwise I'm free. Perhaps we could have lunch. Becky has already shown me your appointment book."

"That would be lovely," Dana murmured carefully. "Just give me a few minutes to freshen up. It's been quite a morning."

"Which you handled beautifully I'm sure." Mocking, angry, loving. It was the most seductive voice she had ever heard.

"Dana can cope with anything," Becky piped up loyally. "Even little kids."

It was absolutely *crucial* Becky said no more. Dana shot her a swift quelling look, which Becky, needle-sharp, caught.

"How is Alice?" Logan asked. "I've brought her a present. I'd like to give it to her in person."

"I'm sure you will." Dana felt another wave of guilt and anxiety. Why hadn't she contacted him last night? She was angry at herself. She deserved what was coming. Logan hated being kept in the dark.

They lunched in a riverside restaurant on baby lobster with a piquant lime sauce followed by coral trout. It was delicious but Dana was so nervous she left most of hers.

"What's the matter?" Logan asked with raised brows. He let his eyes move over her, feeling the pull of attraction, too deep, too threatening. Still he had called on her, never managing to keep his emotions under control. He loved the sleek simplicity of her pale suit, the beautiful silk blouse beneath. He had always admired her dress sense. He had never seen her look anything less than stylish in whatever clothes she wore. But it wasn't simply her beauty that gripped him, it was the slender grace of her body, the way she sat and stood, the colours she wore, the meticulous grooming. She radiated a quiet confidence. Today she looked the successful professional woman she was, but a weight loss was apparent and her lustrous skin had a transparent look, as though she was working herself too hard.

"I'm not all that hungry, I'm sorry," she apologised.

"Are you sure all this dedication to your career is worth it?" he asked dryly.

He would have to know sometime. "It's not exactly my career, Logan." Dana raised her eyes to his, met them fully. "There's been a whole chapter of disasters lately."

"Meaning what?" His answer came swift and clipped, just as she expected.

"I'll tell you, but please don't lose your temper."

Narrow-eyed, he sat back. "It's something to do with Melinda, of course. Has she been giving you and Alice a hard time?"

Now her sense of being in the wrong swelled to huge proportions. "There's no easy way to put it, I'm afraid. Melinda's gone."

"Gone?" His tone bit.

"As in, took off," Dana explained with grim humour.

"Don't tell me with Alice?" Logan asked through clenched teeth.

A waiter approached them, took note of their expressions and immediately backed off.

Dana reached for her wineglass, took a long, calming sip. "No. Melinda left for London all by herself."

"I think you'd better tell me the whole story," Logan suggested in a tone that made her wince, "and don't leave anything out. I knew from the look of you something has been weighing pretty heavily on your shoulders."

"I don't think we should discuss it in the restaurant." Dana's eyes made a quick circuit of the luxuriously appointed room. Several women were staring at Logan with undisguised interest.

"So where would you suggest?" He lifted an arm, signalled the hovering waiter for the bill.

"I want your promise you won't get angry."

"That may be tricky."

"Logan, you look dangerous!" she said, and meant it.

"I might be if you don't get around to telling me," he warned. "Where is Alice? At school?"

Dana could see what was in store for her. "She's staying with a friend of mine. A lovely person. Alice is in good hands."

"Let's get out of here," he said with exasperation.

They went to her apartment to have their long overdue discussion.

"Would you like some coffee?" Dana stalled as they entered the living room.

He whirled her around, compelled her to face him. "Don't act as though you're frightened of me. That's not you, Dana."

His closeness totally rattled her. He was a passionate man. The tight self-control was more a necessity. "I'm ashamed to say I'm in awe of you, Logan. I always have been."

He made a sound of disgust. "Let's talk. We can have coffee later."

So the whole story came out. Logan listened in silence, making a visible effort not to intervene, though anger showed in his eyes.

"Aren't you feeling a little ashamed of yourself?" he asked finally.

She nodded. "I wanted to ring a dozen times but something always got in the way. We didn't exactly part the best of friends. I'm not such a fool I didn't know that. I've been thoroughly occupied trying to keep up with my commitments and looking after Alice." She couldn't mask her hurt.

His handsome mouth twisted and he stood up, pacing to the doorway that gave onto the balcony. "Whatever is between us shouldn't have stopped you. You only had to make one call and we'd have given you all the help you needed. Taken Alice off your hands. If she needs some counselling it can be arranged. There are no obstacles that can't be overcome."

"No, but there's a whole lot of disarray while you set about tackling the problem. Please sit down again, Logan. You remind me of a prowling tiger."

"Good," he said shortly. "Now you just might walk more carefully around me."

"Surely I've always done that?"

"That's interesting." He turned on her. "Tread carefully yet lure me on at the same time?"

"Is that how it looks to you?" Dana spread her hands, looked down at her ringless fingers.

His eyes gleamed. "Damn right! Only I'm not good at playing games."

"Really?" Their fragile truce was splitting wide open. "You don't hesitate to step over the edge."

"Only with you, Dana," he said very quietly. Too quietly. He moved with coiled energy to where she sat, coming behind her as she sat on the sofa, letting his lean strong hands encircle her slender throat. "I want so badly to believe in you,'' he said with a curious mixture of sadness and hostility.

"Haven't you ever heard of an act of faith?'' She shuddered convulsively as his hands slid down over her shoulders to her silk-covered breasts.

"Maybe I'm too suspicious a man.'' There was pain now in wanting her. Real pain. The force of it shocked him.

"You would rather allow your doubts to warp you rather than follow your instincts?''

"If I followed my instincts right now, you know what would happen.'' His voice registered a hot sensuality.

"Oh, I do,'' she said bitterly, and sprang up, her skin flushed, her eyes deep and dark. "Whatever you want you get.''

"You played your part, as well,'' he charged her, his voice hard now. He wanted to pull her to him, fold her in his arms. He wanted to connect with her at the deepest level, but he heard Melinda's voice in his head, too. Even despising her she had only said what his own family believed. The spectre of Tyler would always be there to haunt them.

Watching him, Dana smiled grimly, suddenly feeling humiliated. "I can't bear much more of this,'' she confessed. "Perhaps we shouldn't see one another at all.''

"Did you switch on for Tyler, Dana?'' he flared.

She threw up her hands. "That's it. The big question! Nothing I could say would convince you otherwise. If you'd like a cup of coffee I'll make it. God forbid, I should keep you from your appointment.''

In the kitchen Dana moved quickly, even though her hands were trembling with emotion. To be alone with Logan in this mood was enough to drive her frantic. She was pouring near boiling water over the fresh coffee grounds when Logan moved into the kitchen, instantly charging the atmosphere. It was like all the overhead lights had been switched on.

"Black?" she said stormily when she knew perfectly well. Black. Two sugars.

"I'm sure you know the answer to that." He curled his fingers into his palm, exercising the tight control he had long used around her.

Her lashes were low, sweeping her cheeks. Her hands, like his, weren't quite steady. Next thing he knew the glass coffeepot was skidding along the counter and Dana was crying out.

"Ouch!" Hot coffee had splashed over her hand, causing an instant red stain. Quickly he grabbed her, propelling her towards the sink where he turned on the cold water.

"That must have hurt."

His concern, the sudden tenderness in his voice, quite undid her. "It's all my fault. So stupid." She was trembling all over.

"No, damn it, it's mine. I've upset you. God, I'm a brute." He continued to hold her hand under the cold running water. "Most of it has gone over the bench. It could have been a lot worse. Poor baby."

Why these lightning transformations from accuser to lover? They were nearly destroying her.

"Dana." He put his mouth to the sensitive skin behind her ear, moving her back closer so they were body to body. "Want me to kiss you?"

Desire. The warm oblivion of it. "No." Her denial was pathetic, little more than a whisper.

"Liar." He lowered his dark head, his mouth trailing gently down her cheek.

She lost herself in sensation. Her head fell back against his shoulder and though she kept her arm extended as though on automatic, she lost all sense of injury and the running water.

"I can't help but want you," he murmured, desire and a kind of despair deep in his voice. Maybe some things in life were best left alone. Past relationships. His arms wrapped her completely now, his mouth moving over hers with incredible hunger, capturing it, claiming it for him alone.

She was so physically vulnerable to him. Sheer ecstasy shot through her. Rapture to glory in. She hadn't thought it possible to need a man so much; hadn't thought it possible the depth and abandonment of her own response. Her will was so fragile, melting under the force of his. How had he ever learned so much about her? How had he arrived at such a level of intimacy as though he knew her body as well as his own?

Her head was beginning to swim as passion drove deep. Only a kiss, and her sensuous nature was released. The longer his mouth held that kiss, the more her body yearned. She wanted his hands and his mouth all over her. She wanted that matchless passion even as she realised she might never have his love. These moments for him were a form of imposed blindness.

His long lean fingers were laced into her hair, his body almost supporting hers as she leaned into him, helpless to deny conquest.

"What do you do to me?" he muttered against her throat. "I'm crazy about you. Want it or not."

That element of male hostility had her struggling away from him. "Chemistry I think it's called." Even to her own ears she spoke raggedly.

"And an awful lot of it. Maybe too much for a man to handle. I don't just want to *kiss* you, Dana. I can tell you that." He leant forward, turned off the tap. "Here, show me your hand. I hate to see those red marks on your beautiful skin."

"Don't fuss," she almost shouted, no longer able to act normally.

There was a faint pallor beneath his dark copper skin. "All right. Take it easy." He spoke soothingly, as though women were as fractious as horses. "I don't want you hurt, Dana," he said, his dark timbered voice deep and serious. "I don't want to be hurt, either."

CHAPTER SIX

IN THE following weeks Dana was overtaken by a recurring sense of emptiness and loss. It was almost like a darkness had fallen on her. The urgency of her work propelled her along, nevertheless she was terribly aware something altogether vital was missing from her life. She and the Dangerfields were bound together. She missed Alice greatly. She had become very used to having her little goddaughter under her wing, but through all her thoughts, flamelike, ran Logan. The tragedy was she had allowed that flame to burn her. She had even begun to fantasize about having him for a husband. Logan to share her days. Logan to share her bed.

For the first time in her life she was having trouble sleeping, and even when she did, it was only to have that impossible, unattainable man stalk her dreams. Why had she ever allowed him to make love to her? It had so profoundly changed everything. Logan's lovemaking was all she seemed to think about. Even when she closed her eyes his image moved like pictures behind her closed lids. To lose him now would cut her to the heart. Jimmy and Melinda between the two of them had cost her Logan's trust. Logan thought a great deal of trust. He would demand it totally of the woman he loved. She truly knew what it was to be the innocent victim and it made her ache.

Ainslie rang weekly to keep in touch, always allowing Alice to speak, Alice's words tumbling over each other with her excitement. No reproaches from Ainslie. Dana had brought her granddaughter closer. Nevertheless Ainslie told her privately Alice had reverted to a few

difficult moods and the occasional tantrum which rather
shattered the overall harmony. Only when Logan was at
home could the household be assured of no discord.
Alice's emotions were not yet in balance. She seesawed
between sunny periods and days of wilful behaviour that
required a lot of love and patience. She was missing
Dana dreadfully, Ainslie said. Dana was a pivotal part
of Alice's life.

"We're all looking forward to having your company,
Dana," Ainslie told her warmly. "I'd love it if you
could see your way to coming to us *before* Christmas.
Some days I desperately need your support. Sandra
spends so much of her time with Jack. My disciplining
skills have blunted over the years, I'm afraid. My heart
aches so for Alice, I should be a little firmer. Logan, of
course, charms her. She's a little angel with him."

Dana could believe that perfectly. Though Sandra often took over the phone for a chat, Dana had no contact
with Logan. It was Sandra who gave her the news
Phillipa had taken to dropping in at Mara. She was pi-
loting her own plane now, a single-engine Cessna, a
magnificent birthday present from her wealthy pastoralist
father.

"I think she's dying to start up with Logan again,"
Sandra confided. "There's no other man in her life and
there's been no other serious relationship for Logan. I
don't know how he feels about Phillipa now but I can
tell you for a fact she's still in love with him."

Just hearing it made Dana's blood run cold. It was
never clear to her why Logan and Phillipa had split up
in the first place. Any man would be happy to marry
Phillipa, she thought. Everything about her was calm,
confident, controlled. She was good-looking in a healthy,
athletic way, not glamorous like most of Logan's ex-
girlfriends, but well turned out, attractive, a fine companion for the owner of a grand station. She could just

bring it off, Dana thought. Phillipa was far closer to what Logan really wanted than she could ever be. Phillipa could never be accused of having had an affair with the tragic Tyler, either.

In the end Dana didn't send Logan an invitation to her solo showing. In one way she desperately wanted him to see her work, admire her artistry and professionalism, in the other she was unwilling to put herself through the torture. So emotionally buffeted she had taken shelter in the calm waters of isolation. Encounter could only bring ecstasy and anguish. The sense of loss would go on forever. How to survive without Logan was going to prove one huge ongoing problem she had brought on herself.

On the evening of her showing, which took up a whole floor of the prestigious Stanford Gallery, Dana dressed to the nines. This was going to be a very social evening. One couldn't do without the "glitz crowd," not that they ever bought anything, but their very presence added glamour and excitement to the occasion. The serious people from her own world would be there and art collectors looking to wider fields. Colin Stanford, the gallery owner, had rung her earlier in the day to tell her two representatives from overseas galleries had flown in especially after the gratifying reception of her work at the Venice Biennale. Both representatives were from commercial galleries like the Stanford, one in Berlin, the other in New York. It would pay her to impress not only with her artistry but her personal presentation. As one of her colleagues put it laughingly, "the whole package."

Tonight she wore a short slip dress of dark chocolate taffeta covered with exquisite black lace. She always looked good in black. It went well with her hair and skin and the gleam of the taffeta gave the whole outfit an additional lustre. Because the dress called attention to her legs she had invested in a pair of beautiful Italian evening shoes worn with the sheerest of black stockings; gold and jet drop earrings, an antique shop find, her hair a long ash-blond slide. Always light-handed with her makeup she set to a little extra colouring and sculpting so in the end she thought she looked rather exotic. Certainly glamorous enough to fit in with the ultra-chic crowd.

When she arrived the gallery was already so crowded Dana thought anyone who was seriously interested in her work would have to come back the next day when the gallery would be near empty. Colin Stanford rushed forward to greet her, delighted she was looking so absolutely "smashing," something he couldn't take for granted with a lot of his artists. Taking Dana by the arm, he introduced her around, beaming fondly while she was offered a whole lot of compliments. The men were delighted to meet her, blondes always were the centre of attention; the women, either envious or impressed, seemed more interested in what she had on than the wide range of photographs expertly placed around the walls. The showing had a name: "Journey of Life." It featured images from the moment of birth, through childhood, adolescence, the courting years, marriage, midlife, old age, on one's own or in nursing homes, the inevitable images of dying and death. It was a serious body of work. Dana had put her heart and soul into it.

While the champagne and finger food were being circulated and the hum of conversation had reached such a high level the air itself was turned to noise, she was approached in turn by the two overseas representatives who seemed genuinely excited by her work.

"So young to know so much about the human condition," the gentleman from Berlin murmured, seizing her arm to discuss a booking.

The American in the next ten minutes, not to be

beaten, offered to "buy up the whole showing." "Australia's too small my dear," he told her. "You have to exhibit in the States."

It sounded as though she was quite a success.

Long-time friends swelled the ranks, people she had known since college days when she had studied film-making and had even made a couple of documentaries and a short film that had received quite a bit of attention. Gerard and Lucy arrived, delighted at the brilliant showing, hugging and kissing her.

"I always knew you'd make the big time," Gerard told her with pride and pleasure. Though he loved his Lucy dearly, Dana would always have a place in his heart. Everyone knows about first love. One never entirely gets over it.

Logan, who had waited for an invitation and deemed it perhaps unwise to accept, found himself reacting badly when one didn't arrive. This was throwing down the gauntlet indeed. And how it stung him! The past month he had found himself toiling through his days with a lack of enthusiasm that was entirely new to him. He had managed his life so much better before he had allowed a woman to slip into his bloodstream exposing his all-too-apparent vulnerability. His life up to a point had been rife with good-looking girls. He had even become engaged to Phillipa whom he had known all his life.

Phillipa was bright and attractive, suitable in every way. She understood thoroughly his way of life and enjoyed it, but he had learned the hard way Phillipa could be as disloyal as the next one. While he had been away on a trade mission to South-East Asia, Phillipa had spent the weekend with an old boyfriend who was still crazy for her. She had claimed later, weeping copiously, it had been just "one of those things." They'd been to a rock concert. She'd had too much to drink. But loyalty shaped his life. He didn't want a woman who could fall into bed so easily. He also became uncomfortably aware he had never loved Phillipa in the first place. Maybe it was all his fault. Phillipa had become aware of his true feelings and sought comfort where she could. In any event, they agreed to break off the engagement. A mutual decision. He didn't want to be taken over by love. He had far too many responsibilities.

His strong feelings for Dana Barry had always disconcerted him. Not only was she extraordinarily beautiful, she was extraordinarily gifted with a warm, giving nature. She aroused such sensations in him, strange hungers that gnawed at him long after she left and Mara was his own again. The relationship seesawed constantly before the sharp winds of doubt. A kind of self-sabotage and mostly on his part. Never a man to waiver, he wasn't doing too well now. The trouble was, he could never reconcile himself to a reality of Dana with Tyler. He has always thought her, for all their complex dealings, absolutely straight. He hated himself for even suspecting her, but he couldn't unload the burden of evidence.

Except for that time in the cave. There all the barriers had been swept aside as their bodies reached a sublime harmony. She had been perfect to make love to, filling him with such pleasure, such a sense of wholeness, he felt the Bible was right. She was his Eve, his missing rib. Was this intense passion something to be seized on rather than cause alarm? It was the end of peace. He knew that. The end of his peace of mind. When there was important, even dangerous work to be done, the image of Dana got between him and the project. In a way it was like leaving one's borders undefended. Maybe this was the way Tyler had felt. Captive and confused. Dana Barry was a crisis in both their lives.

No one challenged him when he arrived at the gallery. He wasn't asked to show his invitation. He simply

walked through the door, not stopping to think his whole
aura assured him of automatic entry. Why would a man
who looked like that ever have to gatecrash anything?
One or two even stopped him, trying to gather him into
their circle, but he smiled and said he was anxious to
view the collection. A futile pursuit, he thought, when
the crowd was so huge. Were any of these people genuine buyers or were they simply being seen before going
on to the theatre or dinner.

In the end he stood back, as much away from the
crowd as possible, seeking out Dana. He knew she was
successful, of course. He knew she was very good. Over
the years he had seen quite a lot of her work, which was
becoming far more meaningful as she matured. His interest was genuine.

"Super stuff!" a distinguished man said as he walked
past. American, from the accent.

A small section of the crowd moved suddenly, heading en masse towards the photographs which were beautifully lit and displayed. It was then he saw Dana and
something like elation rose in him on a wild wave. Their
coming together the way they had, had opened up the
floodgates so his whole world looked different and he
found himself moving in a strange new landscape. He
continued to stare at her, spellbound.

She was the most wonderful-looking creature he had
ever seen, beautiful as were others, but so full of life, of
sparkle. The laughing, chattering crowd moved around
him but he felt compelled to stand and stare at her. She
was looking highly polished and sophisticated in a way
he had never seen her. Tall on her high heels, beautiful
black-sheened legs. The dress was exquisite. Suddenly
melancholy, he remembered how well black suited her.
The black suit she had worn the day of the funeral. She
was laughing at something an attractive young woman
said as she hugged her, obviously a friend, adjusting her

gilded waterfall of hair before a young man captured her, kissing her cheek soundly then holding her by the shoulders, looking down smilingly into her face.

Hell, the guy was in love with her. Their whole body language was far from casual. They knew one another well. For an instant he felt an unprecedented surge of pure jealousy, which only abated as he saw Dana move back, her expression full of an affection which embraced the young woman, as well.

So he was wrong after all. Just as he could be very wrong about Dana and Tyler. The seeds of doubt once sown spread tenacious tentacles.

A moment later he felt a touch on his arm, dissolving a moment of anguished struggle.

"Good Lord, Logan, what are you doing here? I thought you'd be back on Mara, pulling your weight for the country."

"Good evening, Sir William." Logan turned, smiling to acknowledge the handsome, elderly man at his side. "Actually I know Dana Barry very well. Have known her for some years. Her cousin Melinda was married to my late brother."

"Terrible business." High Court Judge, Sir William Hardy, shook his pure white head. "I'm so sorry, Logan. It must have been a great blow to the family."

The two men stood in conversation for a few more minutes before a colleague sought the judge out. Much as he liked and admired Sir William, Logan had kept his eyes trained on Dana all the while as she spoke to the changing crowd clustered around her. She was obviously very popular with the kind of vibrancy that drew men and women to her. She was very gifted, as well. Now he could see the photographs more clearly as some of the crowd left to go on with their evening. Another twenty minutes or so and he would be free to study the collection in detail.

And then she saw him, her colour deepening with a rush of astonishment, excitement, whatever. It didn't take her long to reach him. "Logan!" she said quickly, almost breathlessly, presenting her perfect cheek for his kiss that wasn't social at all. "Why do you always confound me?"

"It's nothing really," he drawled, blue eyes blazing. He wanted to pick her up in his arms there and then. Carry her away to the quiet opulence of his hotel suite. Make love to her until she lay rosy and satiated in his arms.

"I'm absolutely delighted you've come!"

He heard the warmth and excitement in her voice, revelled in the transparent joy in her face.

"How could I refuse your personally worded invitation?" He smiled with that part of him that mocked.

"I did *want* to but I was afraid of... Oh, I don't know—" She broke off. "Anyway, you're here and I'm absolutely thrilled."

How could he doubt it when her beautiful eyes, tender and velvety as a doe's, sparkled with pleasure?

She took his hand, her tumultuous feelings for him gathering force, introducing him around with great pride. Everything about him made her heart beat faster, made her feel more alive such was the power and vibrancy he generated. Others felt it, as well. She saw it clearly stamped on their faces.

"You must come and meet two very dear friends of mine," she invited him, brushing her long gleaming hair out away from her creamy neck. It was a trick that tantalised him, making him want to put his mouth to her satiny skin.

Lucy and Gerard Brosnan.

Gerard. The name cut through him. The ex-fiancé. Now he had it. His instincts were never far out. The young woman, his wife, was pretty, with short dark hair, vibrant green eyes, and a pair of engaging dimples in her cheeks. An attractive creature but no Dana.

"They all love you, don't they?" he murmured as eventually they moved off.

"I'm a very lovable person," she joked, a little thrown by his tone. She knew, none better, Logan was a man of strong passions, but she had never seen him exhibit the faintest trace of jealousy.

"One wonders what you saw in Gerard as pleasant as he undoubtedly is." He bent to her ear.

"Perhaps it had something to do with the fact he's not in the least like you. Phillipa, too, has moved on." She felt a strong desire to add, "It appears now she's back," but that would be giving Sandra away. Better by far to keep that inside information to herself.

"Will you let me stay with you tonight?" he asked abruptly in an extremely taut tone.

She had to remind herself forcibly she was on full view of the crowd. Even then her whole body trembled as though she was on the verge of a high fever.

"We both know, Logan, that would be a mistake."

"I want to touch you. I want to make you shiver with ecstasy. I can't seem to get the last time out of my head."

His voice was so sensuous, so rich and deep, it was almost like being made love to. She could feel her whole body quickening, the shooting, piercing little thrills, the startling tightening of her nipples.

"Logan, stop," she whispered.

He took her hand, brushing her with delight. "Don't close me out."

It was the nearest Logan Dangerfield would ever come to begging. She was so excited. On top of the world yet full of confusion that flowed around her like floodwater. She knew the sting of his mocking tongue. She knew the whole range of emotions she incited in him. The underlying hostilities. The deeply implanted doubts.

"Please come and look at the collection," she said, and gave a little involuntary shiver. "I don't know that I can cope with any more than that."

He laughed deep in his throat, so vividly, vividly alive. There was never any doubt for either of them about what would happen.

The day before she was due to fly to Mara, a long letter arrived from Melinda. Dana sat in her living room for a long while turning it over before opening it. Something about it made her feel physically and emotionally drained. She had done far too much trying to fit all her commitments in before taking off. Now this. Finally she sighed and, using a small silver letter opener, slit the envelope neatly.

A whole store of memories of Melinda came back to her. None of them pleasant. When Melinda had abandoned her child, Dana felt her days of covering up for her cousin were over. There were few surprises. Melinda wrote endlessly of herself. How these days she was looking so good she was turning heads. She had met a lot of very nice people who had "taken her over," showing her a good time. She was wearing her hair differently now. Several lines to describe this. She was wavering about cosmetic surgery. No matter her weight loss she still had a trace of a teeny double chin. In fact she had had one since childhood. A negligible thing. Not even unattractive. She had met someone very interesting only that week. A lot older but someone rich and cultivated. Someone high up in the city, a stockbroker.

Just as Dana was beginning to wonder if Melinda would ever mention her daughter, Melinda advised she had sent early Christmas messages off to the family. A letter each for Logan and Ainslie. A very expensive card for Sandra, "Never did like her, looking down her long nose at me." A magnificent life-size doll for Alice when Alice wasn't a doll child at all. Surely Melinda knew that. "Max and I picked it together." Melinda was just beginning to find herself, fighting out of the trauma of her disastrous first marriage. Obviously this meant she contemplated a second. "A door has closed behind me, Dana," she wrote. "I'm starting a whole new chapter in my life. Maybe I can find time for Alice later. I do love her, you know, but there's so much of the Dangerfields in her."

Thank God, Dana thought.

She didn't want to read any more but felt she had to. "I hope you've forgotten about Logan," Melinda added a warning. "He's the type to find second-hand goods distasteful."

Dana flinched. *Second-hand goods?* Did anyone say things like that anymore? Truth and lies. Melinda didn't know the difference.

Dana rose with a passion, tearing her cousin's letter into shreds. Why had it taken her so long to realise Melinda had never wanted her to find happiness? Perhaps it was a kind of madness? Melinda had coveted everything she ever had. She remembered that now. For the first time in her life Dana began to seriously contemplate a child might be better off without a certain kind of mother. A mother utterly insensitive to her child's needs.

CHAPTER SEVEN

THE charter pilot was brisk, businesslike, directing her to one of the rear seats of the Cherokee Six. There were four other passengers, twin boys of around fourteen, old hands at air flights, on their way home for the long Christmas vacation, a very tense elderly man with a clipped moustache who was visiting his sons, and a middle-aged woman with an attractive friendly face returning to Teparri Station where her husband was head stockman. This was after a two-week visit to her sister in the Big Smoke which was still the Outback name for beautiful, bustling, cosmopolitan Sydney. They all began talking to each other in easy Outback fashion except for the elderly gentleman Dana had privately labelled "The Major." The pilot made another quick round of external checks then shut the baggage doors hard. A moment more and he climbed into his seat, glancing over the flight plan.

"Wow, aren't you lucky!" the boys said when they found out she was en route to Mara. "Dad took us there once to watch a polo match. Mr. Dangerfield's team won, of course. He's a great player," Chris, the elder boy by ten minutes, told her, "the homestead is out of this world. Compared to Mara, Dad said our place is a tin shed."

"I bet you love it all the same," Dana smiled.

"It's home." Chris sighed in a happy holiday-time voice. "Can't wait to get there."

Mara was the last stop, the most remote. On Teparri the Cherokee taxied along the strip towards the hangar, braking to a stop just before a boundary fence. Mrs.

Harrison disembarked and waved. Now Dana was on her own. It had been an uneventful trip, clear blue skies, no rogue air currents to lift the aircraft up and down like a yo-yo, which sometimes happened, but tiring. Logan was to have come for her, picking her up at the domestic terminal but at the last minute had to change plans to make an urgent visit to one of Mara's outstations.

Dana was dozing lightly when the pilot's voice reached her, calm but very decisive. "Listen, I want to put down. There's no need to be alarmed. It's just a precautionary check."

Dana jerked forward so suddenly her seat belt cut into her. "There's nothing wrong, is there?" As used as she was to light aircraft, indeed enjoyed flying, she was perfectly aware there was always an element of trouble and danger.

"Just something I don't think I should ignore. Call it instinct. I can't actually see anything wrong. All the needles are pointing the right way. It's just a feeling. I'm very sorry, Miss Barry, but it's best to err on the side of caution. The plane's a bit sluggish."

"Well, you're the boss," Dana said doubtfully. "Where are we?"

"Our exact position is twenty-five miles south-west of Teparri Station. I'm sending a message now to Flight Service to announce my intention to land," the pilot said. "If I *have* to, I'll arrange for our engineer to be flown in. If we flew straight on we'd be over Mara in about forty-five minutes. With any luck at all there should only be a shortish delay. One of the wires might have come off the pulleys. Or—" He broke off, by this time almost talking to himself. "It's the oil pressure. The gauge is dropping."

It was on sunset before Logan flew into Mara, asking his overseer, Manny Buchan, who was waiting for him, if Miss Barry had arrived.

"Not as yet, Boss," Manny answered in his usual drawl.

"What?" Logan, who had begun walking to the waiting jeep, turned back on him sharply.

"What time was she supposed to be here?" Manny asked, surprised by the boss's reaction. He looked shocked and then anxious.

"I would have thought four o'clock. Run me up to the house, Manny. There may be a message."

"Hop in." Manny took the wheel with alacrity. He'd been caught up most of the day supervising a muster so although he knew Miss Barry was due to arrive that afternoon, he hadn't heard when.

At the homestead, Ainslie came out to greet him, her expression matching his own. "Dana hasn't arrived as yet. I'm starting to get worried."

"Did you get onto State Aviation?" Logan referred to the charter service.

"I was just about to when I heard the jeep. You do it, dear." Ainslie's voice sounded strangled in her throat. In truth she was seized by a panic that had never left her. She had lost her husband, Logan's father, to a fatal plane crash over which she was still agonising. Flying was a way of life in the vast Outback but it was never without its fatalities nor would it be.

Logan more than anyone knew the dangers. His father had been a very experienced pilot, as he was himself, but that hadn't helped with mechanical failure. In his study he got through to the charter service who at that point didn't know the plane was overdue. It took ten minutes before they were notified by Flight Service in Brisbane the pilot had advised them of his intention to land but there had been no subsequent confirmation the aircraft had landed safely. A search flight would have to be organised.

It wasn't enough for Logan. Fierce anxiety rushed through him. Never a man to panic, he realised his heart was thudding. His strong features drew together, giving him a very daunting demeanour. The fellow at the other end kept talking, explaining the situation, but he found himself chopping him off, telling him as an experienced pilot he intended to start the search himself. The only remaining passenger on the Cherokee was a member of the Dangerfield family which was to say close to God in that part of the world. The thought of Dana out there in the desert was tearing at his insides. It was too soon to think of anything else.

At that point Alice, who had broken away from Ainslie, ran into the study causing him to almost jump at her high-pitched yell.

"Where's Dana? Where's Dana? Is she going to be killed?"

Logan slammed down the phone, caught the child and lifted her in his arms. "Alice you'll have to quit that racket. Where did you get that idea?"

"I heard Retta tell one of the girls the plane was long overdue," Alice choked.

"Well, you can stop worrying right now," he told her firmly. "The pilot had to put down. Just a precaution. That means he was being very careful. He radioed his position, south-west of Teparri Station. You know Teparri Station. It's not all that far from here. I'm going out to find them now."

"Really? Aren't you wonderful. Can I come?"

"No, you have to stay with Grandma and I don't want any fuss," Logan said. "I'm going to bring Dana home."

"I can't help being frightened, Uncle Logan."

"I know, sweetheart." He kissed her cheek. "If you like you can wait up, though it might take a while."

"Oh, yes, *please*," Alice breathed in a fervent little voice. "I couldn't sleep anyway. I can't even remember a time when I didn't love Dana. Do you believe in God, Uncle Logan?" she asked, her child's gaze very direct.

He nodded, keeping control over his own apprehension. "I believe in a Divine Being, yes."

"He wouldn't let Dana get lost," Alice said.

He was airborne just after dusk, flying into a night sky already peppered with stars. Mercifully he knew this part of the world, vast as it was, like the back of his hand. He had the charter flight's last recorded position. The pilot had notified Flight Services he would let them know when he had landed safely. No further transmission had come through but that didn't necessarily mean a crash. He had to hold on to that. There was another scenario. The pilot couldn't contact Flight Services on his VHF on the ground. He would be out of range and he mightn't have checked his high frequency radio before take off. He prayed to the God Alice so staunchly believed in that was the case.

Dana. She was never off his mind. Why hadn't he gone for her? It had been the plan. Now he wished with all his heart he had put the outstation's problems on hold. In a blaze of new knowledge he realised he loved her. Had loved her for some time even when he was crippled by doubt. An image of her slipped into his mind. The image when she was last in his arms. Her beautiful eyes full of magic, her mouth curving, her long gleaming hair spread out over the pillow, her body so warm, so sweet, so silken, desire tightened in him even then. Dana had transformed his life, now the thought of her mortality cut through him like a knife. On odd occasions in the past he had thought himself a man of stone so controlled were his emotions. It was a measure, in a way, of how he had been brought up. Responsibilities, a big heritage, the untimely death of his father, the disaster of Tyler's marriage, then the terrible news that had brought a hard lump into his throat. Men didn't cry. They were trained not to. It was only underneath they took the full brunt of their losses.

Losses?

God, what if...?

When he saw the lights of the charter flight he cried aloud with relief. Shouted at the top of his voice. No crash. His entire body relaxed and his formidable strength flowed back. How strange and extraordinary to find these feelings in himself. The crazy thought that without her he would most likely die? Him? Whose whole life was duties and commitments? No wonder the immense power of these feelings made him fearful.

He landed the Beech Baron on a track baked so hard it was almost as good as a landing strip.

Dana swooped to him, arms wide open like wings. "Oh, Logan!"

He gathered her to him, held her painfully fiercely close, struggling not to kiss her senseless. "What the hell do you think you've been up to, frightening the life out of me?" he demanded, feigning exasperation.

"All I can say is you've found me." She lay her silky head along his chest, feeling the texture of his khaki bush shirt against her skin, her ear attuned to the strong beat of his heart. "Not hurt, either."

"Thank God." His voice was deep and quiet. "Hello, there. Dangerfield," he introduced himself to the pilot who approached hand outstretched.

"I remember your dad well." They shook hands. "Never had the pleasure of meeting you. It's damned good of you to come." The pilot taciturn, but always polite, began to open up to another man. "Trouble with

low oil pressure,'' he said. "Tried to get a message out
when we landed. No problem with that, but my H.F. isn't
working. My fault, I'm afraid.''

While the two men walked back to the Cherokee still
in conversation, Dana walked over to Logan's Beech
Baron which was resting like some giant wide-winged
bird on the desert track. She had known, of course, they
would be rescued but she hadn't fancied a night under
the stars with a complete stranger, correct as he was.
Now Logan had come for her. He really was a knight in
shining armour. In *some* ways, she smiled to herself,
when he wasn't the impatient, impossible oh-so-arrogant
autocrat laying down the law. Just the sight of him made
her radiant. Logan Dangerfield in action was a glorious
sight.

Dana lifted her head to look up at the stars, marvelling
at their infinite numbers, their unique brilliance. The desert air was so pure nothing got between her and them.
A series of images like snapshots flashed across her
brain. She had camped out under the stars only once.
That was when Jimmy was alive and as a special treat
he and Logan had allowed Alice, with Dana for company, to experience how wonderful it was to spend a
night around the camp fire; sleeping out in the wild bush,
along the bend of a billabong. She still remembered the
moment when Logan had bent over to check on her
sleeping bag, asking her if the ground wasn't too hard.
Just an ordinary thing yet as his hand briefly touched
her, her heart had leapt like a fish to the lure. She had
never managed to keep her calm around Logan but at
least her imprisoned heart had kept its secret.

Almost immediately, Logan got a fire going, brewed
up coffee he had on the plane to make them feel better.
He hadn't stopped to pick up food, but he had a few
bars of chocolate and some fruit, which he offered to
the pilot. He'd already offered to fly him back to Mara

but the pilot made the decision to stay with his plane, apologising again his high frequency radio hadn't been in order. Logan had already transmitted the message the Cherokee had been found with all on board safe. He advised further he would be flying Miss Barry on to Mara Station, her original destination. "How do you feel about a night in the desert?" he asked the pilot, who only grinned.

"The desert is my kind of place. I'm a bit of a loner. Anyway another plane will be here in the morning."

"Just stay put," Logan advised.

On the flight back to Mara, Logan said surprisingly little, wanting to keep the force of his emotions tamed. He expected he'd go crazy but he had promised her once there he would keep his needs under iron control. One hell of a promise when he wanted to claim her this very night. Even the thought of it made him groan aloud.

"What's the matter?" She turned her head, seeking the reason for that sort of pain.

"What do *you* think?" His brilliant eyes flashed.

"Logan, I don't know." She touched his arm.

"I'm thinking of laying you out on my bed. I'm thinking of unbuttoning that silk blouse. No hurry. Nice and slow. Then the jeans. I'm thinking of feeling your satiny woman's flesh under my hand, only it's business as usual. Wasn't that the deal?"

She laughed at the brisk change of tone. "I'm almost sorry we made it."

"*Almost?* Even in this light I can see the blush."

"I have to look to my position," she said. "Your position."

"True. You're Alice's godmother. I'm her uncle. Both positions are sacred."

"Have you ever thought of marrying me?" she asked as she meant to, satirically.

He laughed deep in his throat. "I've thought of it dozens of times."

"And?"

"I'm damned if I know how it would turn out," he drawled. That wasn't fair. "We live in different worlds. Your last exhibition really opened my eyes to your artistry. You're still young. You could have the art world beating a path to your door. How could you turn your back on all that?"

"If you're making excuses, Logan, they're working," she replied dryly.

"I mean how could we make the transition from *family* to husband and wife?"

"I never understood how we made the transition to lovers," she retorted sharply, lying through her teeth.

"I'm going to die of wanting you," he said.

Their arrival back at the homestead turned into a celebration, with station staff coming to the door to check all was well. The word had gone out and everyone was anxious. Mara had had enough tragedies. Though long past her bedtime, Alice ran around ecstatic with joy. Finally she sank with sheer exhaustion to the floor, her feet perched on a footstool, her head on a cushion. "Next time I'm going with you, Uncle Logan."

"Next time?" Logan threw back the last of his single malt Scotch, and set the glass on a side table.

"Next time you have to rescue Dana."

"I don't know that I like the idea of *next* time," Logan said feelingly. "Once is enough."

"But wasn't it romantic?" Alice queried happily. "Did you kiss her?"

"Heck, Alice, I didn't have a chance to." He smiled, his beautiful white teeth in stunning contrast to his dark tan. "I hugged her. That's a start."

Ainslie, who was sitting on a sofa, caught Dana's eyes. "Dear girl, could you pour me just a little more champagne? I really want to unwind. I'm no good with worry anymore.''

Logan moved first, on his feet as smooth as a big cat. ''I'll do it, Dana. And you're for bed, young lady,'' he told the excited, yawning Alice, large eyes overbright.

''No thanks. I can't get up. I might sleep here.''

''No way.''

''Carry me,'' Alice cajoled. ''Some nights it seems like half a mile to my room.''

''You will live in a mansion, darling,'' Dana smiled.

''You have to come, too, Dana.'' Alice rose, a little wobbly on her feet, going to her grandmother, kissing her soundly. ''One of these days, Grandma, I'm going to have a little sip of champagne.''

''Happy times ahead,'' Logan joked, swooping his niece up. ''Are you turning in, Ainslie?'' he asked, his eyes on his stepmother's pale face. To his sorrow Ainslie seemed to have aged dramatically since Tyler's death.

''Yes, dear,'' she murmured, followed by a tired little laugh. ''Dana, give me a hand up. I don't think I've ever been so pleased to see anyone in my life.''

After Dana had seen Ainslie to her room, she walked along the wide corridor hung with paintings, to Alice's room. Logan was there, tucking her in.

''Uncle Logan and I are good buddies,'' Alice informed her. ''I like that. Good buddies. And he believes in God, Dana. He told me.''

''You were having a very serious conversation, were you?'' Dana moved to the opposite side of the bed, smiling down at the little girl.

''I was terribly frightened when you didn't arrive.'' Remembering, Alice's eyes filled with tears.

''Oh, darling, that's awful.'' Dana's heart smote her. She bent down and hugged her. There had been too many traumas for Alice.

"Uncle Logan kept my hopes up. He told me I could stay up and wait for you."

"I'm safe. I'm home. And your eyes are drooping," Dana said soothingly. "You get your sleep and tomorrow we can talk all you want. I've got books and games for you and a little camera. I'm going to show you how to use it."

"What about now?" Instantly Alice sat upright.

"Not a chance," Logan said in a firm tone. "I hate the idea of you girls going without your beauty sleep."

That made Alice laugh. She snuggled down obediently, and fell asleep wondering what her first picture would be. Maybe one day she would be as famous as Dana and have her own exhibition.

Out in the corridor once more, Logan caught her hand, determination in his fire-blue eyes. "Let's go for a walk," he suggested. "I want to clear my head."

Excitement soared, looped like a bird. Still she said from behind her perpetual shield, "But what's the time?"

He laughed, a sound so attractive it made her senses swim. "What an idiotic question. Whatever the time, it doesn't matter."

As they walked through the moonlit garden their feet crunching on the fallen leaves, they were serenaded by a solitary bird.

"He's singing his heart out for us," Dana murmured. "Sweet and silvery and sad."

"Then it just has to be a song of love," Logan responded, lifting an overhanging branch out of her way. "Love's an agony after all."

"You really think that?"

A gentle breeze was blowing full of the scent of flowers and the wild bush. "I've had a taste of its power," he returned very dryly.

"Is it something you're going to share with me?"

"I think you're perfectly capable of working it out yourself."

"Well I'm not," she said honestly, breaking off a gardenia and twirling it under her nose.

His voice was crisp and very slightly edged. "I think it's transparently clear I'm in love with you."

The thrill of hearing him say it swept through her like a fire. "But you don't trust me?" she said, a great sadness in her eyes.

"In some ways I'd trust you with my life," he admitted.

"But you can't stop thinking about me with Jimmy?"

"I thought you were going to try to say Tyler?" he responded in the same slightly edged voice.

"Jimmy is how I remember him, Logan. I hope that doesn't upset you too much."

"You know it does. I can't exactly say why. I don't blame Tyler for loving you, Dana. You're awfully easy to love."

"We *are* at war, aren't we?" she said quietly, glad of the fragrant blackness to hide the sorrow of her expression.

"It's like something we can't help. But I'm never going to let you get away."

She took a few moments to speak. "Are you going to allow me to marry or are you going to lay down another one of Logan's laws?"

"Why, do you have anyone in mind?" He sounded utterly certain she didn't.

"I'm twenty-six, you know. I want what every woman wants. I want a husband who loves me as much as I love him, children we can both adore, a home to share. I want a purpose in life. I want to push the boundaries of my self-development as a woman, a human being."

He bent his head, kissed her briefly, a mocking gesture. "I think you're doing very nicely. I've said it before, but you have a considerable gift with your photographic images. You're a true artist."

"I hope to be," she answered gravely. "I have other needs, as well."

"You think I don't?"

"Beyond your basic instincts?"

"That's a low blow. Do you seriously believe what I feel for you is *lust?*"

She shrugged, realising it wasn't. "I know some part of you finds me taboo."

He made a sound of frustration. "Surely it doesn't require much understanding to know I have difficulty dissociating you from Tyler in my mind."

"When all you have to go on is Melinda's lies?" She stopped short and turned to him, raising her face.

"Melinda?" He gave a bitter laugh. "We'll come to her later. I had a letter from her. So did Ainslie."

Dana felt her heart sink. "She wrote me about it. What did she have to say?"

"A whole lot of garbage," he answered bluntly. "I really enjoyed hearing about how she's enjoying herself in London, how she's met a new man. I'd be beside myself only Alice is taking her defection unnervingly well. I thought the disappearance of one's mother, even a bad mother, would cause a lot of trauma."

"Children get on with life," Dana said a little awkwardly. "I had thought she'd be more upset myself."

"But she's confounded us all. Her grief is for her father and she was fretting about you."

"Her father was able to demonstrate his love."

"Melinda's your enemy, you know," he said with deep conviction.

"That's an odd word for a cousin."

"I know it hurts." He brushed her words aside. "For some reason Melinda is flawed. She sent me another warning about you. Of course that's what the letter was all about.''

"All you have to do is ignore it."

"I did tear it up," he said shortly. "Ainslie made a little bonfire of hers. Ainslie has just lost her son and Melinda can't wait to tell her about her new man. She really needs help."

"I'm sorry, Logan. There's nothing more I can do about Melinda. Having one's parents is central to development. Melinda lost hers early. Obviously all we tried to do for her was unappreciated and unwanted."

"One would have to feel sorry for—what's his name?"

"Max. Maybe she's a different person without her stresses."

"Without her child, you mean," he said incredulously. "In the last analysis, Dana, she wants to hurt you."

"That's becoming increasingly clear," Dana said bleakly. "I'm a little tired, Logan. Can we go back?"

"Why don't we just move into the summerhouse?" His voice was both intense and ironic. "I want to make love to you."

"When I don't have your respect?" she challenged.

"Dana, I never said *that*."

"And I believe I said I'd never be your mistress."

She went to turn away from him, suddenly deeply emotional, but he gathered her to him. "Lust corrupts, Dana. What I feel for you is entirely different."

"Then why do you have to punish me for it?" She was truly bewildered.

"Because you make me so damned *miserable* when you're away from me," he protested, his expression for a moment touched with male outrage. "You get between me and my work. What kind of a thing is *that*? I'm supposed to be entirely focused and all I can see is your beautiful face. It's clear to me that's obsession.''

''Well, it must be a real change for you,'' she said tartly. ''You never did tell me what happened between you and Phillipa. Was she giving you a bad time, too?''

''I didn't worry about Phillipa when I wasn't with her,'' he said.

''Have a care, Logan. I think you're admitting you got engaged to someone you didn't really want.''

He laughed shortly. ''You aren't going to tell me you didn't? Anyway that's all in the past.''

''Are you quite sure?'' She was afraid now of losing control.

''What's that supposed to mean?''

''I think Phillipa's heart is still in your hands,'' she retorted fiercely.

''Dana, our relationship is over. Why on earth are you mentioning it?''

''Maybe Phillipa doesn't believe it. Something about you puts women in a frenzy.'' She stopped abruptly, starting to crumble. Her emotions were more fragile than she thought and she'd had a glass too many of champagne.

''Don't you dare cry.'' He looked down at her intensely.

''Who said anything about crying?'' She heard the rising note in her voice.

''Because if you do... if you do, my God, you'll be lost to me.''

''We can't do this,'' she pleaded, but her voice was no more than a whisper on the wind.

''There's nothing in the world I want more.''

''Wanting isn't the same as getting.'' Even when she was trembling in his arms she employed her defence weapons.

''Is it not?'' He turned up her chin, allowing the moon

to shine down on her face and reveal the liquid glitter of her eyes. There was such a vulnerable innocence about her. Despite the dreadful letter that had made his heart twist inside him, he wanted to believe in her. So *badly.* "I'm not going to let you go without a kiss."

Though she yearned for him, she resisted. But only for a moment. In the end she could deny him nothing. He knew it. She knew it. So when he released her her heart was hammering and her body was profoundly aroused.

"I guess you're lucky I'm a man of my word," he said, anguish in his harsh tone.

To be together now on Mara. On his own land. And so many barriers still left between them.

to stare down on her face and reveal the tanned tiny of her eyes. There was such a vulnerable tenderness about her Dana felt the painful desire that had made his heart twist within him, he wanted to soothe in a very... her flushed face lifted toward him ... found a loss. Though she appealed to him, she resisted, but only

CHAPTER EIGHT

IT TOOK Phillipa less than a day to find out Dana Barry was in residence at Mara. The following day she obeyed the compulsion to fly in, the very picture of friendliness. As far as Phillipa was concerned, her love story wasn't over. She wasn't such a fool she didn't know Logan had never been *mad* about her, but she was in love with him, had always been in love with him and he had been very fond of her.

Logan was the most dynamic man she had ever known, the sexiest, the best-looking, the smartest, the richest, a star of the first magnitude. The same hero he had always been in her mind. That little episode with Steve, nothing really, and she was not promiscuous, had cost her dearly. She had lost Logan's respect though there was nothing cheap or shabby about Steve. Steve did love her and he had asked her many times to marry him. In one way she had always known it was wiser to look to Steve as a life's companion. Steve wasn't complex like Logan, neither was he terribly exciting. Logan was incredibly so and very glamorous however much he would deride the term.

Now Dana Barry with her beautiful face and well-documented talents had moved in. Phillipa had always found her very pleasant, well-informed and interesting to talk to, but she was increasingly disturbed by the thought Dana could present a problem just when she and Logan had made up their quarrel and she was once more in his good books. Of course Logan had never told anyone of her little "slip." She didn't expect he ever would, which was her great good fortune.

Once or twice in the past Phillipa had thought she had discerned a very curious tension between Logan and "the cousin," which was how most of them knew Dana. Nothing very obvious or important. Logan and Dana were both very correct with each other, but a certain atmosphere prevailed so that on hearing the news Phillipa and her mother decided immediately Phillipa had best get over to Mara and size up the situation. Phillipa's mother had been planning their marriage since childhood. The breaking off of the engagement had upset her dreadfully. "How could you have lost him?" There was no doubt in Phillipa's mother's mind Phillipa had done all the losing but Logan was still unattached, lending weight to her theory Phillipa and Logan were destined for each other.

Logan was out on the job when Phillipa flew in, but the women greeted her with a genuine warmth. They all sat out on the veranda enjoying morning tea, with Alice sitting close by reading one of the beautifully illustrated children's books Dana had brought her.

"I thought it was high time we got to know each other better," Phillipa said amiably, leaning back in her comfortably upholstered wicker armchair, watching a couple of groundsmen move around the many-acred garden, bringing down yellowing fronds on the tall palms. It always gave her enormous pleasure to visit Mara, one of the great historic homesteads and such a wonderful showcase. The Dangerfields were vast landowners but Mara was the flagship. It was a compelling enough reason to marry Logan even if he hadn't been every woman's dream.

Mistress of Mara!

Phillipa very nearly cried aloud at her loss. Instead she asked, "How long do you plan on staying, Dana? Long enough to come visit us, I hope?" Phillipa's family, the Wrightsmans, owned Arrolla Station some two hundred miles to the north-east.

"I'd like that, Phillipa," Dana responded lightly. "I'm here until around mid-January."

"No you're not," Alice said, briefly lifting her head. "You're going to stay with me forever."

"But surely, dear, you'll be going back to school?" Phillipa laughed uncertainly, looking towards Ainslie whose expression looked vaguely embarrassed. "And how is Melinda? I expect she'll be joining you for Christmas."

Dana remained silent, waiting for Ainslie to deal with it, but Alice as was her wont, burst in, "Mummy took off. She's over in London now. That's the capital of England where the Queen lives. She's not my mother now. She doesn't want me."

"Alice, darling, would you mind popping into the kitchen and asking Mrs. Buchan for fresh tea?" Ainslie asked.

"Sure, Grandma." Alice put down her book at once. "I expect you want to tell Phillipa all about it."

Ainslie's mouth pulled down. "Thank you, darling."

A brief look of shock passed across Phillipa's cool good-looking face. "Is there a problem?"

"No problem," came Dana's reply, intercepting Ainslie's agonised look. "As I'm sure you'll understand, Melinda is going through a bad time." Dana made it sound convincing. "She wants some quiet time to herself. Somewhere far away."

"Yes, of course," Phillipa murmured, her agreement tentative. Whoever heard of a mother leaving without her child? Of course the marriage had been a disaster. Everyone knew that. "So does this mean Alice will be living here for a while?"

"She's looking on it as a great adventure," Dana said. "And she desperately needs her family."

"You, too, by the sounds of it." Phillipa's gaze shifted constantly from Ainslie to Dana as though looking for some break in a united front.

"Well, we're family, too. Alice is my goddaughter as well as my second cousin. I've been looking after her for a long time."

"She's a dear little thing," Phillipa murmured when she didn't think so at all. She had seen Alice in one of her tantrums with no one in the house outside Logan able to handle her. Ainslie, always a robust woman, was looking almost frail, obviously grieving for Tyler. She wasn't up to looking after a difficult small child, Phillipa thought. Sandra was spending more and more time with the Cordells. In-laws one day. "I haven't seen any of your photographs, Dana, but I read in one of the papers your recent showing was a great success."

"Yes, it was." Dana smiled at the memory. "I'm really thrilled at the public response."

"And she's had wonderful offers from overseas galleries," Ainslie said proudly. "Logan was telling me all about it. He was immensely impressed."

"Logan?" Phillipa showed a glimpse of shock.

"He went to see it, of course," Ainslie said.

"When was this?" Phillipa's lightly tanned skin took on a rosy hue.

Here we go again, Dana thought. "He came to the gala opening," Dana informed her.

"Really? Well, he kept that a secret."

"Was he supposed to have told you?" Dana smiled slightly.

"It probably slipped out of his mind," Phillipa said, shrugging a straight shoulder. "I'm envious, of course. I never can take a decent photograph. Don't have the time really."

"I intend to take hundreds while I'm here," Dana said, excited at the prospect. "I want to make my own contribution to recording this unique environment.'' She didn't mention some of her best photographs had been used in a conservation battle.

''But surely—'' Phillipa gave a little smile ''—with all due respect, Dana, there are scores of books on the Australian wilderness? Mumma has dozens. All the coffee table variety.''

''But I have my own way of looking at things, Phillipa. That's the point. The photographer's individuality. Great photographers are great artists. I want to make my way.''

''I'm sure you will,'' Phillipa hurried to say. ''I know Serena wants someone really good for her wedding but I expect she would be fixed up by now.''

''Thanks, Retta,'' Ainslie said in a rather tired, sweet voice as an aboriginal girl, as graceful and small-boned as a bird, moved out onto the veranda bearing a tray.

''I'd love to do a series of pictures on our aboriginal women,'' Dana said, making room for the tray, and greatly taken by the beauty of Retta's hands.

''I can help you there, Miss Dana,'' Retta said.

''I'm counting on that, Retta.'' Dana smiled.

In the end Phillipa stayed all day and was invited to spend the night just as she expected. It was the routine. Dinner would furnish her with the opportunity of observing Logan and Dana together. Dana appeared to be genuinely devoted to the child, spending the afternoon entertaining her with lessons on how to use a camera, while Phillipa herself went in search of Logan, finding him rounding up clean skins at Cudgee Creek. This was Phillipa's world. She had been born and raised on a large station that ran both sheep and cattle and she was very knowledgeable about all aspects of station life. A prerequisite she had always thought for becoming mistress of Mara. Logan might have a great eye for beauty but he was very hard-headed when it came to making the big decisions. And marriage was the biggest. Dana Barry with her extraordinary silver-gilt hair and contrasting velvety brown eyes was essentially a creature of the big cities. Maybe she might even make the move to the United States if she was that interested in furthering her career.

As it happened, Sandra returned home early, before lunch, with Jack Cordell in tow, throwing her arms around Dana and hugging her. Something that Phillipa found a mite disturbing. Although she and Sandra, who was several years younger, always got on, they had always stopped short of demonstrations of affection.

They had finished a highly enjoyable shooting session with Alice's brand new Olympus MJU, a compact and robust little camera, basically point and click but with excellent results. Now they were resting under a beautiful old ghost gum on a hilltop that looked down on a panorama of flower-strewn slopes and flats, the results of one of the late afternoon storms that worked up with great thunderclouds and little passing rain just a short week before. The flower displays that after good rains could turn into blinding displays of pink and white paper daisies were a vision that could never be forgotten, but the Spring rains had been unpredictable with only isolated falls. Songs and prayer chants had already begun for the longed-for rainy season linked to the northern monsoon when the desert wilderness turned into the greatest garden on earth. Still Alice was happy to photograph the bush that she loved, a goanna resting on a log too lazy to move, three brolgas standing in deep conversation beside the silver bend of a billabong, an obliging aboriginal stockman leaning against a gate holding his horse by the rein, and a desolate pile of rubbish and mortar that long-ago sheltered stockmen touched some artistic nerve in her.

"Thank you, Dana," Alice said, softly touching her godmother's cheek. "I love my camera."

"I'm so glad, darling." Dana was indeed pleased with Alice's vision, enthusiasm and quickness of mind. "I'm hoping this might be the start of a lifetime interest. I started very young." She leaned back and opened the picnic basket they had brought with them. "Fancy a sandwich?"

"Yes, please." Alice accepted one gratefully. "I'll have my drink now, as well."

"This is marvellous, isn't it?" Dana sighed with contentment, leaning back on a cushion. "A glorious place if you have an eye for the wild, vast, open spaces under a perpetual cobalt sky."

"It's our home," Alice said. "Mine and yours."

"And Uncle Logan's." Dana laughed. "He's the boss, so we can't forget him."

"It was Uncle Logan who said it." Alice sipped her home-made lemonade through a pink and white straw. "I think that was lovely of him."

"I agree." Dana's heart melted. "I didn't think he would include me."

"Well, he did. He likes you a whole lot better than you think," Alice pronounced owlishly. "Phillipa doesn't have to come here anymore, does she?"

Dana broke off part of a cookie and put it in her mouth. "Why's that, darling? The family have known her since she was a little girl, just like you."

"Is that why she and Uncle Logan got engaged?" Alice leaned over and plucked an iridescent little beetle from Dana's collar, admiring it then placing it gently on a leaf.

"He may have loved her perchance," Dana tried to joke.

"I don't think so." Sometimes Alice was given to enunciating very clearly, just like her grandmother.

"And what would you know, young lady?"

Alice rolled her eyes. "Give me a break. If you love someone so much, why do you have to hide it?"

"Meaning?" Dana turned to her, startled.

"Kissing and stuff. Hugging. When Uncle Logan speaks to her, he just sounds kind. I thought he might be in love with you."

"Oh, man," Dana sighed. "How did you figure that out?"

"Simple." Alice put out her hand for another sandwich. "His eyes light up. They go all blue and sparkly like Grandma's big sapphire. And he *sounds* different."

"You're really smart."

"Yes," Alice agreed complacently. "Kids are a lot smarter than grown-up people think. I don't think Phillipa likes me."

"I'm sure she does," Dana responded instantly. She didn't like Alice to be hurt. "Some people are better with children than others, that's all."

"No, she doesn't like me, Dana," Alice repeated. "It's all right. I don't akshly like her. I heard her asking Mrs. Buchan once if I was the naughtiest girl in the world?"

"And what did Mrs. Buchan say?" Dana looked into the big, gold-flecked hazel eyes.

"You bet!"

At that they both broke up.

Because the afternoon was so hot they drove to one of the many beautiful lagoons that formed a network all over the station, leaving the open jeep on the plain and walking down the narrow, winding slope to the moon-shaped pool. Here the calm cabochon waters glinted with a million sequins, with islands of deep pink lotus lilies glowing like sculptures on the sea of green floating pads. Hundreds of golden bottlebrushes and wild gardenias grew close by, spreading their delicious scent over the entire area and filling their lungs. Anticipating just such a swim, both of them had worn their swimsuits beneath their clothes losing no time peeling them off and folding them in a neat pile on the back seat of the vehicle.

Just as they were about to enter the water, Alice caught at Dana's fingers. "Don't go into the deep, Dana," she said, a little catch in her voice.

"Of course I won't." Dana, busy plaiting her hair, stopped to reassure her. "I would never do anything to upset you. You know that."

Alice nodded, brushing her fringe off her face. "Mummy thinks its terrible I can't swim properly. After all, I'm nearly seven."

"Darling, you'll be able to swim a whole lot better by the end of the holiday," Dana promised. "Mummy was expecting a little too much of you."

"She's terribly good, isn't she? Almost as good as you."

"We had our own pool at home, Alice, and my father coached us a lot. I'll give you some lessons in Mara's swimming pool. Now we're going to have fun."

They sported without incident for the best part of an hour, revelling in the open air and pure cold water on their heated skin. This was a timeless place, an oasis of quiet calm, sustaining a wide spectrum of birdlife. Above them a black falcon soared majestically, wings outstretched forever in the search for prey and, undisturbed by their presence, a pair of brolgas began to wade out to the succulent waterlilies on their lofty, stick-like legs.

Afterwards they spread their towels on the honey-coloured sand, their bodies protected for the most part by overhanging green boughs.

"Do you miss Mummy, darling?" Dana asked, concerned despite all that had happened Alice didn't appear to be missing her mother at all or perhaps was bottling up her grief.

"I do sometimes," Alice confided, turning to look steadily into Dana's eyes. "She's Mummy even when I know she doesn't want me."

So small and so brave. So much the victim of Melinda's lack of love and understanding. Sometimes Alice broke her heart. Dana tried to find the right words. "We have to remember, like you, Mummy was frightened and lonely after Daddy died. She needs time to find herself, to adjust to a new life."

Alice sighed deeply. "But she told Daddy she hated him. They had a big fight. It was *terrible.*"

Almost moaning in her grief, Dana reached over and took the little girl's hand. "I'm so very sorry you had to hear that, Alice. But I'd like you to think of this. Sometimes when they're upset and angry, people say things they don't mean. I know you will understand that!"

"You mean, my tantrums?" Alice said immediately in her intelligent way.

"I mean when you're upset and confused. When we sob and rage, it's a protest about something. It means you're not satisfied. Probably Daddy had done something Mummy didn't like. Telling him she hated him was just a reaction, like you tell people you hate them and want them to go away."

Alice frowned, remembering. "I've never said that to *you*, Dana."

"Oh, yes, you have, my girl. Lots of times." Dana tickled her.

"I never ever meant it. You're always lovely to me, Dana. So different from Mummy."

Dana's feeling of regret was enormous. "We'll have a long talk about it, darling, when Mummy returns."

If she *ever* returns, she thought dismally. It was a good

thing most women weren't so woefully deficient when
it came to loving kindness.

"So this is how some people spend their day?" a
familiar voice, pitched loud enough to reach them,
called.

Alice stared back, then jumped up excitedly.

"Uncle Logan, Uncle Logan."

"Hi, sweetheart." He flashed her a white smile.

Now another figure emerged. Phillipa, looking a little
bit hot and bothered. Logan reached back a hand to her
and in another few moments they were down on the
sand.

"Are you going to have a swim, too?" Alice asked,
so put out by Phillipa's unexpected appearance her voice
held a trace of wrath.

Phillipa laughed sharply. "Not today, I think. I don't
have a swimsuit."

Her cheeks began to burn. Oh, this was upsetting indeed! And it had only taken one look. One look to turn
a pleasant acquaintance into rivalry. When had Logan
ever looked at her like that, his blue eyes blazing? It was
like a blow to the stomach. Not that she could ever look
as good as that in a purple bikini. Not given to envy,
Phillipa felt a great wave of it.

Dana, not unaware, came to her feet, her long ash-
blond hair sliding out of its loose plait and cascading
over one shoulder. Emotions were palpitating in the air
like actual heartbeats. "That's a pity," she managed
lightly. "It's absolutely beautiful in. The water's surprisingly cold." She, too, had caught Logan's look, the
blue-fire eyes, the slight flaring of his finely cut nostrils.
She realised, too, Phillipa was disturbed, and no wonder!
Logan wasn't supposed to look at her like that, but for
once his reaction had been unguarded or maybe he didn't
care.

Alice came to their rescue, grasping her uncle's hand.

"I'll have all these great photos to show you, Uncle Logan."

He smiled down at her, pleased she was looking so much better than when she had arrived pale and pinched. "So Dana's started you off already?" he asked

"Aren't you glad she did?"

"I sure am. Anything that makes you happy makes me happy. It was very nice of Dana to buy you a camera. I wish I'd thought of it."

"But surely she's too small to use one properly?" For an instant, cool, confident Phillipa couldn't contain a sudden flair of hostility. Something that really shocked her.

"Not at all," Dana answered smilingly. "The one I bought her is excellent for a beginner. Alice is very intelligent and she has a very good 'eye.' I'm very pleased with her. What have you two been doing?" Dana only glanced at Logan, wishing she had at least brought her pink cotton shirt down with her. Never a self-conscious person she now felt extraordinarily aware of her own body and the amount of cleavage her bikini top was showing.

"Doing the rounds, the usual old thing," Logan offered casually, blue gaze flowing over her. "Pip always shows a great interest in Mara."

"It's my favourite place," Phillipa gushed, pleased Logan had reverted to her old nickname.

"Don't you like your own place better?" Alice asked in a vaguely belligerent voice.

"Of course I love it!" Phillipa glanced down at this horrid little girl. "But bless me, it's not Mara. I don't know anything to equal Mara."

"Someone should take you to Kinjarra, or Main Royal, or Bahl Bahla," Logan mocked.

"The devil's in you, Logan," Phillipa said.

"Thanks a lot."

"It only makes you more attractive."

Dana privately agreed. "So, will we go on home, Alice?" she asked. "Sandra will want to see you."

"Nah, not with Jack around," Alice said, startling them all. "They're sort of mad about each other, aren't they?"

"One is supposed to be when one intends to get married," Phillipa began rather piously only to then blush a bright red.

"One day you'll meet one special guy," Logan told Alice lightly, taking her hand.

"Will I really?" Alice looked thrilled.

"Count on it. I'd say you're going to make one heck of a woman"

"Like Dana." Alice smiled.

Phillipa moved off, striding it out. Half an hour ago she'd been happy. Now she was down in the doldrums, wishing Dana would go back to where she came from.

Dana tried to keep up, but she wasn't wearing shoes and her city feet were very tender. Logan and Alice were a little distance behind her, Alice straggling to protect her bare feet, as well. The track was harder to negotiate going up than down, the sandy earth covered with leaves and twigs and seed pods, abundant little scurrying insects and isolated masses of delicate yellow wildflowers.

"Why don't I carry you?" Logan suggested to Alice.

"Not unless you want to break your back," Alice chortled. "No, I'm okay, Uncle Logan."

"How's it going, Dana?" Logan called, wanting to trap her in his arms. The light was dancing over her beautiful skin. She moved like she was dancing. She had a dancer's lovely strong but delicate legs. That neat little butt just made for a bikini. He could see the slight swing of her small perfect breasts as she bent suddenly, putting her hand down as if to steady herself.

"Ouch!"

They all heard the little sound of pain.

"Dana?" He left Alice's side, moving swiftly, efficiently, up the slope. "What is it?" He grasped her around her bare, narrow waist, bringing her upright.

"Damn. After such a delightful day I think something has stung me."

"Hang on one minute. Just one minute." He moved back to Alice, swinging her into his arms and carrying her to the top of the slope.

"It's probably nothing, Logan." Phillipa frowned, for a moment considering. "A bull ant." When had he ever acted so concerned about her?

"Dana doesn't normally react like that," he answered a little shortly.

"I don't think it's a bull ant, either," Alice said.

"Okay. So what is it? She'd know if it had been a snake."

"It can't be a snake," Alice said with great intensity.

"Next time you'll remember to wear your shoes," Phillipa responded with faint censure.

Alice glared at her but had the sense to keep silent.

Logan reached Dana in half the time it took him to ascent. "Here, hold on to me while I take a look. Where is it, your foot?"

"Yes, the soft part underneath." She was speaking calmly but her foot had started stinging badly.

"You really should have worn shoes. It's always best to take precautions."

"I know, I'm sorry." She laughed a little shakily, reacting to the closeness of his body, his warmth and his strength. "It could have been Alice."

"That must be painful." He held her slender foot in his hand. "A bee sting probably. All the bottlebrushes are in flower. The bees love the nectar. You trod on one or a couple by the look of the swelling. Only other thing is a spider. It's certainly not snakebite."

"I'm pleased about that." Dana's tone was dry.

"There's not a damn thing I can do about it until we get you back to the house."

"I'll survive." She fought down the instinct to reach out to him. Instead she tried to put her foot down.

"What the hell!" Logan stared at her for a long moment then lifted her as easily as he had Alice, into his arms. "You're one lovely creature, Dana Barry. I could carry you for miles."

"The trouble is, I need my clothes."

"Not by me." He gave a provoking little laugh. "That's what comes of being a hot-blooded male."

"Oh, yes?"

"Shall I prove it?"

"Not with *Pip* around."

"Why don't I just kiss you and be done with it?" His gaze touched her, sizzled.

"That seems monstrously cruel."

"Maybe," he agreed.

"Are you alright, Dana?" Alice called anxiously.

"Of course she's alright." Phillipa was dismayed by her own grumpy voice. "Don't worry, dear, Uncle Logan to the rescue."

"He practically loves Dana," Alice said.

For an instant Phillipa felt close to screaming. A remarkable thing for her.

"That is a shame," she clucked sympathetically when Dana showed them the fiercely red, swollen area. "As I've just said to Alice, it's wise to wear shoes, but then, you haven't spent a great deal of time in the Outback have you, Dana?"

"Nonsense, she's been coming out here for years," Logan clipped off. "Listen we'll all go back in the one jeep. I'll send someone back for the other. Dana needs some tea tree oil on that sting and a painkiller."

"Oh, my, what's the fuss!" Phillipa laughed lightly,

watching Dana shoulder into a pink shirt, buttoning it modestly over the creamy swell of her breasts. "I rode in a cross-country race once with a broken collarbone."

Dinner made Phillipa even more uneasy. Because there were only six of them, they used the informal dining room which flowed on from the breakfast room adjoining the kitchen. Not that there was anything too informal about it, Phillipa had always thought; a large dark-panelled room illuminated by day with tall leaded windows, a Venetian glass chandelier by night, a huge tapestry on one wall, a matching pair of consoles with mirrors above them on the other, a long refectory-style English oak table with two magnificent oak carvers at either end and eight chairs. Because there were guests there were a series of silver candlesticks with tall lighted tapers down the centre of the table, with a low crystal bowl of yellow roses in the middle.

The Dangerfields were used to living grandly so much so it was bizarre to think just outside the main compound was a great wilderness, as savage as it was splendid and beyond that the Simpson Desert spreading its vast intimidating presence over an area of 15000 square kilometres. Sandra, though she was still grieving deeply over the loss of her brother, had picked up, Phillipa thought, and with Jack to stay, joined in the conversation that ranged over a wide area: local news, the political situation, various hotly debated issues and Dana's highly successful show.

"It must be so exciting for you, Dana, to be invited to New York?" Sandra smiled across the table, looking for a moment so much like Jimmy, Dana had to look down quickly so as not to show her feelings. "You'll go?"

"Of course she will!" Phillipa interjected, wanting

nothing more. "It would be so exciting, no artistic person would think of giving up the chance."

"And all the showing sold." Sandra showed her genuine delight. "Now I can boast about you to all my friends. Fancy having an international audience for your work."

Think about that, Logan cautioned himself, his eyes on Dana in her exquisitely soft green dress. Was there no colour she couldn't wear? He knew, first-hand, dealers had been vying to get hold of her work. She had sold every last photograph that evening, in the end to the American dealer because he intended to keep the entire show together.

"After all, you can only go so far here," Phillipa was saying. Almost like a prompt.

Dana twisted the stem of her wineglass, knowing what Phillipa was about. In a way, feeling sorry for her. "My work is really about being an Australian, Phillipa. It's *my* country and *my* way of looking at things."

Phillipa had to force a smile. "I think you'll change your mind once you get to New York."

New York, Logan thought. A world away. Almost another planet. What did an Outback cattleman have in common with a photographic artist on her upward climb to the top? Her talent would get her there. Her beauty, like a lily in bloom, would assure her of a public image. The whole world admired beauty and talent.

Jack Cordell, who had a secret desire to beat Logan at billiards at least once, dragged him off for a game. Logan had tried to cry off but in the end gave in good-naturedly. He had plenty of paperwork to get through and a proposal from a pastoralist colleague to consider a partnership venture, but he always tried to get in some relaxation and he liked Jack. He had known the Cordells all his life and he approved of Jack as a husband for Sandra. Jack was a fine young man from a well-respected family and he was always on hand to give Sandra the kind of comfort and support she needed.

Once the men departed, the women retired to Ainslie's large sitting room. It was a beautiful "blue" room with an entrancing painting of a tree in a green field against a densely blue sky above the mantelpiece. The painting alone was so real it transported the viewer to the green meadow. Dana loved it and the combination of sofas, armchairs, fabrics, a few wonderful antiques and the tall bronze lamps. It was a room as distinguished and restful as Ainslie herself.

They chatted for some time, listened to Ainslie's classical CD's, then Dana excused herself saying there were a number of things involving her studio she still had to attend to. Although she had worked intensive hours to clear her commitments she still had letters on hold which she would now send by fax.

"You'll look in on Alice, would you, dear?" Ainslie said. "It took her such a long time to go off."

"Excitement." Dana smiled. "Don't worry, Ainslie, I'll attend to it."

"I've been no help." Sandra apologised for her absence. "I've needed to be with Jack but I'm going to get closer to my little niece now she's here. I must say she seems a lot happier than I supposed under the circumstances."

"When did you last have word of Melinda?" Phillipa came a little too near to demanding.

It was Ainslie who answered, slowly, reluctantly, acutely aware of Phillipa's disapproval. "Just recently. You must remember, Phillipa, Melinda is a woman in shock."

"She's the most selfish woman in the world, you mean," Sandra burst out, then, catching Dana's eye, apologised. "Sorry, Dana. I know Melinda is your cousin, but she makes me furious. I can't understand how she can do this to Alice.''

"Please let's drop it, dear," Ainslie begged, unwilling to discuss family matters in front of Phillipa. Though she had always liked Phillipa, liked the way she was so active in community matters, she had never found her particularly tolerant of failings in others, and her mother, though a bright energetic woman, was a great gossip. Time had to go by before any of them would know exactly what Melinda's plans were for the future.

In her room, Dana drafted a few letters, took her shower, put on her nightclothes then padded down the corridor to Alice's room. Alice was lying quietly, two hands locked beneath pink cheeks, her breathing easy. She looked fine, lightly tanned and healthy. Dana moved the night-light a little further away from the bed. The light was very soft but it was falling across Alice's eyes. She resisted the impulse to kiss the little girl's cheek in case she woke her up, going to the French doors that led onto the upper balcony and catching the gently swaying curtain back into its silk rope.

The night sky was blazing with stars, the sky itself tinted a marvellous dark purple. She ventured out onto the veranda exulting in the warm darkness, the wonderful scents of the bush that rose over and above the more familiar perfumes of the garden. Mara was an incredible place. It had been her first experience of a great Outback station and one that would never leave her. All this was Logan's. Had been his from birth. In a way it was like being born a prince. And tragic Jimmy! To have died so young and so far from home. Now he would never leave.

Dana was just about to turn away from the door when a woman's voice, low-pitched but urgent, reached her from the terrace below.

"How much punishment must I take?" It was

Phillipa, and she sounded deeply upset. "I told you it meant nothing. A mad moment. I'm sick with shame."

It was no surprise when Logan responded, "Why are you bringing all this up, Phillipa? It's over."

It was time to move yet Dana was rooted to the spot, her better judgement way off.

"I can't accept that. How can I?" Phillipa, so cool and contained, responded passionately. "It seems to me with a little forgiveness on your part we could get back to what we had before."

"*Were* we so happily engaged?" Logan asked, and his voice sounded dismayingly cool.

"You know we were," Phillipa protested. "We were meant for each other from the outset."

Logan's laugh was brief and cynical. "So as soon as I turned my back you fell into Steven's bed?"

At this point Dana moved back, in the process stubbing her bare toes against a sandstone pot containing a lush golden cane. Shock acted as an anaesthetic. She couldn't believe the impeccable Phillipa with her holier-than-thou manner, had taken such a wrong turn. It would have been funny only the consequences had been disastrous, dashing Phillipa's hopes and dreams.

"You've heard this a hundred times before," Phillipa pleaded. "It was a mistake. We both had too much to drink. God, Logan haven't you ever made a mistake?" she cried.

"Plenty of them." His tone was hard. "But I'm a great believer in fidelity. Anyway, it doesn't matter anymore."

"But you haven't found anyone else." Renewed hope sounded in Phillipa's voice. "Tell me, Logan, I have to know."

Logan was silent for a few fraught seconds as though measuring her claim. "I don't see it that way at all."

"It's not Dana, is it?" Jealousy distorted Phillipa's normally attractive tones.

"Why would you say that?"

On the veranda above, Dana's face flamed.

"She's very beautiful," Phillipa said wretchedly. "I know how much you prize beautiful things."

"Surely you don't think that's all there is to Dana?" he asked. "Beauty?"

"All right, she's interesting." Phillipa considered shortly. "I've always liked her, unlike that ferocious little pussy cat of a cousin. But Dana Barry isn't the right woman to have by your side," Phillipa said with strong conviction. "On her own admission she's a career woman. She belongs in a different world, not out here."

Logan sounded so taut it was nothing short of hostile. "I appreciate that, Phillipa."

I can't bear this, Dana thought, her frozen limbs unlocking. She began to back slowly, stealthily, towards the French doors, not wanting her movements to be heard nor to wake Alice up.

"It would be awful if you allowed her to disrupt your life." But Phillipa was so upset she was forgetting to keep her voice down. Almost at the door, Dana stood stock-still, desperate to hear Logan's reply.

"I hope I can handle that myself, Pip, with no help from you," he said curtly.

"But I love you. I loved you long before she came into our lives." Phillipa's voice was less audible. "Doesn't that mean anything anymore?"

"This is insane, Pip." Logan's tone was final. "Insane, and I wish you'd stop."

If only Phillipa had, but she was clutching at anything. Things she wouldn't normally have said. Taboo things. "How can I when I feel so *betrayed,*" she cried. "I'm not the first woman to lose her man to Dana Barry."

The air started to shimmer before Dana's eyes. She

felt dizzy, disoriented. It was all her own fault. In listening had she really believed she would resolve her own dilemmas? What was coming would be worse by far. She knew it in her bones.

"What about her relationship with Tyler?" Phillipa challenged in a burning rush.

"I beg your pardon?" Most people would have shrunk from Logan's tone but Phillipa gave a distraught laugh.

"We all knew the marriage wasn't perfect. How could it be with someone like Dana in the background? Why she showed her cousin up at every turn."

"So?" Logan's rasp cut her off.

"A blind person could see Tyler was in love with her." Phillipa's voice was unnaturally clear. "I was a guest here at different times."

What is happening to me? Dana thought.

"You're not so different from your mother, are you?" Logan accused cruelly. "Endlessly in search of gossip."

"I'm clearer eyed than you," Phillipa burst out just as fiercely, her nerves frayed. "My only interest is *you*."

Dana felt a desire to cry out her innocence, but who would listen? She moved back into the bedroom, standing shaken beside Alice's bed. It was just as well children slept so soundly, so clearly had the voices floated upwards. She was nearly weeping herself with pain and frustration, causing her to put a hand against her mouth, swallowing down hard against the tears. All the hoping and praying in the world weren't going to change the fact they all believed in a terrible triangular relationship between her, Melinda and Jimmy. Jimmy could have put things right, but Jimmy hideously was dead. Melinda *knew* the truth, but Melinda these days was filled with a terrible desire to hurt people. For any young woman to marry Logan Dangerfield would be considered a triumph, a splendid match. Melinda was going to make certain that didn't happen to Dana.

It all went back to sibling rivalry on a scale Dana had never dreamt of.

In a flash of recall Dana remembered her cousin as a child, pretty as a porcelain doll with her apple blossom skin, blond curls and big blue eyes. She remembered clearly, keenly, how her heart had gone out to that little cousin so tragically bereft. It seemed to her now she had fallen over backwards all her life trying to make excuses for Melinda, yet she remembered the times they had cried together locked in one another's arms, their tears mingling. Some subterranean part of Melinda did love her. It had showed itself from time to time. So how could she have ever imagined Melinda could turn on her with such venom?

When she finally moved out into the corridor Dana had to stop abruptly, heart hammering, as she saw a lean, powerful figure silhouetted against the pool of light from an open doorway.

"Dana?"

She wrapped her arms around herself in a futile attempt to protect herself from the overwhelming magnetism that never failed to grab her.

"I was just checking on Alice." She flushed, attempting a matter-of-fact tone and failing dismally.

"So what are you shivering for? It's a hot night," he challenged.

Strongly, purposefully, like a panther on the prowl, he began walking towards her. "How much did you hear?"

No mercy from Logan. "I don't know what you're talking about." Absurdly she lied.

"The hell you don't. You were on the veranda weren't you?" He looked down at her, a hard excitement spiralling up in him at the sight of her. How huge were her beautiful eyes, glittering as if on the verge of tears. How pale that lovely face. Desire jabbed at him so painfully it was like a knife point at the heart.

She scented the wildness in him. "Please, Logan. It's late. I want to go to bed."

"No, Dana. I'd rather you talked to me." He pulled her back against the wall. "I knew you had to be there. I could *feel* you. I could even pick up your scent."

"I'm sorry." There was nothing more she could say. "I was looking in on Alice. I had no idea anyone was on the terrace."

"But once you heard us you stayed?"

"I made that mistake, yes." Her chin came up. He had never seemed so formidable or so tall. "I didn't want to, but I couldn't move."

"And I bet you're sorry?" His laugh was low and harsh.

"Don't you think it best if I went to bed?"

"And which bed do you belong in?" he asked.

She didn't think. She didn't repress her blind anger. She was swamped by it. Logan's sardonic tongue laced with honey or gall. She struck out at him, breathing hard and furious, her fists clenched, the force of her emotions staggering in their intensity. So this is what it was like to love? To hate? Their mutual sexual hostility was never far beneath the surface.

"You want to hit me. Go on. Don't bottle it up." He taunted her, letting her flail at him, the blows landing with a satisfying thud on his wide shoulders or the hard wall of his chest. "I could use some kind of fight. Only you're hardly a match, are you?" Then his arms were pining her, his hands moving restlessly, ruthlessly, over her lightly clad body. "How do you think I can hold tight to promises when I feel like this?" he rasped.

"I don't know," she answered bitterly. "Since when did you have time for fallen angels anyway?" She tried desperately to keep her traitorous body under control but it was too avid for his.

"Twenty four hours a day, Dana," he gritted. "That's a helluva lot."

She continued to struggle, fighting down her own weakness.

"What? Didn't Phillipa convince you?" she shot at him, ramming her fists against his chest, trying to put distance between them only she might as well have tried to push back a brick wall.

"What made you do it? I mean…God, Dana." Stifling a violent oath, he grasped a fistful of her silky hair, dragging her head back so his mouth could plunge over hers. Whatever she had done the sheer power of his passion undermined his will, sending it spinning away into space. This wasn't the magic they had known in the cave, or that night they had spent at her apartment. This was treacherous, overwhelming, threatening desire. He could stand no more, his jagged emotions sweeping over him like a flash flood.

She was trembling so badly she thought her knees would buckle. She was shrinking from him yet wild for his touch. She was two people. The woman who loved him, and the woman who couldn't bear his disbelief in her. A disbelief impossible to fight. Only as he took her mouth with such all-conquering passion, the woman in love found supremacy, the other Dana, the victim, moaning with the pain of it all.

He placed his hands on both her breasts, cupping them in his palms, then he bent, lowered his body so he was kneeling, drawing her to him so he could kiss her through the layers of filmy fabric, plunging his face against her, breathing in her body scents.

The excitement of it was so tremendous, her body felt incandescent. Finally she could no longer stand. She pitched forward overcome by ungovernable sensation, her blood in a ferment, her nerves frenetic.

He rose to his feet, lifting her so she slumped over his shoulder, like a rag doll he was holding.

"Logan...Logan..." was all she could say, her voice in an agonised whisper of sorrow, of protest, of an answering compulsive desire. She had to stop him. This one time at least.

Only Logan came to his senses. "I'm going to beat this," he said, and his strong voice shook. For once she was entirely in his power, but it gave him no satisfaction. Holding her captive like some pirate of old, he carried her to her room, throwing her down on the bed so tempestuously her body and mind whirred with reaction and her hair flew wildly around her head in a silver-gilt cloud.

"I won't hurt you if I can help it," he gritted from behind clenched teeth.

She grabbed for his hand and struggled to keep hold of it. "Then start believing in me," she begged, a pulse pounding away in her throat.

"I'm not the damn fool you think I am," he said angrily, pulling his hand away, his eyes in the lamplight blazing like sapphires.

"Okay," she said miserably, feeling utterly defeated. "I'm leaving. I mean that."

His dynamic face hardened to granite. "If I don't want you to leave, Dana, you *don't*."

"You think you can keep me a prisoner?" she said bitterly, trying to sit up.

"You know I can."

And so he could. "I've always been afraid of you, Logan," she said, feeling the cold steel of him.

"I guess I've always been afraid of you, too. With good reason." He bent, kissed her again, so hard it pushed her head right back to the mattress. "Anyway,

Alice needs you. Don't you remember? Her beautiful angelic Dana. Not the Dana who inflames men.'' With a violent movement he pulled away from her, away from the sight of her, her skin flushed, her eyes so dark and disturbed, her light robe that seemed to have lost its sash thrown back from her body, covered in a mere wisp of some creamy silk material. She looked so delicate, so mesmerizing, her nipples erect against the feather lightness of her nightgown, the long skirt of which had wrapped itself around her, pulling taut across her body, exposing her beautiful slender legs the sun had flushed with gold.

He was hideously humiliatingly aware of his own driving hunger. It bordered on agony but he forced himself to control it, tightly coiling his fingers into the calloused palms of his hands. He had never felt so smothered by desire. So smothered by a woman. And the worst part of all. The worst part...

With one galvanic movement Logan moved back from the canopied bed a fine beading of sweat breaking out on his dark copper skin. He could master it. He could master it. He was his own man.

"I can't stand the thought of another day with you," Dana cried, sick with love of him.

"Ditto, my lady." He had recovered sufficiently to manage a hard sardonic drawl. "This just isn't the right time to do anything about it, though, is it? Christmas is coming, remember? The season of peace on earth and good will to men. Everyone is enjoying having you here with the possible exception of yours truly, but then you're not making things exactly easy. Tomorrow I thought we might put up the Christmas tree. For Alice, of course. At least we both love *her*.''

CHAPTER NINE

THE next morning Dana, unwilling to face the day, tried to sink back into sleep but it was too late. She was awake. Early morning sun washed across the room in a wave of bright golden light and bird calls were ringing again and again, carolling across the many species of beautiful native eucalypts that grew in the garden. She lay still on her back feeling the emotions of the night before pressing down on her. How could she carry off the rest of this holiday with Logan feeling the way he did? And all because she had tried to be there for Jimmy when Alice was the real object of her love and attention. She had done everything she could to deny it but there seemed no way to counter the damage. She might even have difficulty trying to explain the situation to an outsider. Where there was smoke there was fire, they would probably say. It was a classic example of mud-sticking.

Dana threw back the bedclothes, moving through the small dressing room to the pretty adjacent bathroom with its Wedgwood blue and white tiles. She was still shocked by Phillipa's admission she had slept with another man when engaged to Logan. Phillipa had claimed alcohol as an excuse and there was no doubt when under its influence the little devils got to work but the excuse hadn't worked. Had she really thought it would with Logan? Probably Phillipa had thought he would never know, when Logan had tabs on everyone even when he was out of the country.

Poor Phillipa! She shouldn't really be feeling sorry for her but she did. Phillipa was a woman who would use every weapon when under threat. Phillipa's words came back to her. "A blind person could see Tyler was in love with her." What had made her say that? Jealousy, of course. But had she *really* believed it or was it a wild charge born of desperation? But where had she got the idea? Sandra? Sandra had been so shocked and lost at Jimmy's funeral, her usual sense of discretion hadn't been working. Had Sandra said something for Phillipa to catch on to? I don't really need another person to condemn me, Dana thought.

When she walked out into the hallway, dressed in yellow cotton jeans and a white tank top, her long hair pulled back into a cool knot, Phillipa chose exactly that time to emerge from her room.

Dana felt like bolting, making a return rush for her room but Phillipa had already seen her. She, too, was dressed in jeans and a pink shirt, dragging on a packed bag and leaving it just outside her door.

"I always said there was a great deal more to you than met the eye." Phillipa lost no time addressing Dana directly.

"Good morning, Phillipa," Dana responded. Keep calm. Keep cool. Phillipa is leaving. "Is there a problem?"

"I'm not sure it matters anymore," Phillipa answered in a bitter tone. "I never realised it before, but you and your cousin are two of a kind." She strode up to where Dana was standing, her eyes pink and puffy as though she'd been weeping.

"Are you going to explain that?" Dana asked quietly, thinking this time she'd have to put Phillipa straight.

"I'd be happy to." Phillipa gave a discordant little laugh. "Both of you went after the Dangerfield men. Your cousin caught Tyler by getting herself pregnant. It shouldn't take you long to achieve the same objective."

There was a sudden chill in Dana's voice. "You're getting very personal, aren't you, Phillipa? Offensive, too. I can see you're very upset but I'm not prepared to listen to this kind of thing. Your engagement to Logan is long over, so you're getting into something that isn't even your business."

"Of course!" Phillipa seemed to be trying to hold herself together but failing. "You don't cheat on Logan Dangerfield. No, sir. If you do you end up in Outer Mongolia."

"I'm sorry, Phillipa," Dana said, dipping her head, trying to balance pity and anger.

"*You're* sorry?" Now it was Phillipa's turn to stare. There was obvious sincerity in Dana's voice.

"I know what the pain of rejection is like." After all, she had been rejected last night.

"Well, well," Phillipa mocked. "I appreciate your concern, but only for *you* Logan might have come back to me. Then you had to arrive with your sparkly hair and your big brown eyes. You're as dangerous to my happiness as you ever were to your cousin's."

It was a monument to Dana's control she didn't cry aloud. "You're talking *scandal,* Phillipa," she warned. "You're talking character assassination. Mine as well as Jimmy's."

Phillipa's gaze went cold and triumphant. "I never said anything about Tyler. *You* did."

"I didn't intend to overhear you and Logan talking last night, either," Dana flashed back.

"An eavesdropper. Was it worth your while?" Phillipa asked contemptuously.

"I didn't know about Steve. That would be Steven Mitchell? One of the elite circle." Dana thought she deserved it.

Phillipa flushed violently. "I'm hoping you won't pass that on," she said stiffly, totally ignoring the fact she herself was into trading insults.

"No, I won't. I don't have any time for people who

pass on hurtful gossip. I can only tell you this, Phillipa, and I want you to believe it, Jimmy and I *did not* have an affair. The thought never crossed my mind. Not ever. He was married to my cousin. End of story.''

''But there's what Tyler said himself.'' Phillipa shook her head, brooding seriously.

''He never said anything about an *affair*. My God, Jimmy wasn't a liar. A destroyer. Maybe he had deep feelings for me and told his family, but when I think about it, why not? In so many ways he was a lost soul. He was doomed right from the start to walk in Logan's shadow. He never had a proper sense of himself, his own worth. He squandered his gifts and his money. But he was really only looking for love and fulfilment. I grieve to say Melinda didn't offer it to him.''

Phillipa frowned severely. ''We all knew about Melinda. But are you sure you didn't offer comfort?''

''Look at me, Phillipa,'' Dana urged. ''Look right at me. Do you really think I did?''

Instead of looking at her, Phillipa looked off. ''I'm not usually like this, you know,'' she said bleakly.

''There's a lot of pain in you.''

Phillipa gave a wry laugh. ''I guess.'' She reached out spontaneously and touched Dana's shoulder. ''You can have Logan if you want, Dana. Have a great life.''

''Except Logan doesn't want me,'' Dana was driven to say. ''You see, Phillipa, I don't have the necessary qualifications. Like most women, I can't live up to perfection.''

Midmorning hours, after Phillipa had flown out, three of the station hands brought the Christmas tree into the house. It was a specially grown-for-the-occasion casuarina, an annual thing, with the tree to be planted out after. Care had been taken to train the tree as it grew, now the slender grey-green pendulous branches, which naturally mimicked a conifer, showed a pyramid form. A huge sandstone pot had been placed to the right of the staircase in the entrance hall, now the men lofted the earth-balled tree into position.

"Up, up and away!" Alice cried excitedly. She stood within the circle of Dana's arms, her gold-flecked hazel eyes filled with joy. "Doesn't it look marvellous!"

"Wait until we decorate it." Dana hugged her. "Grandma has the most wonderful ornaments. They've been in the family for generations."

"This suit you, Miss," one of the men, the ginger-haired Bluey, called, willing to put it wherever Dana wanted. The top of the stairs if need be.

"That's fine, Bluey. Thank you. It's been beautifully grown. So much a part of this desert environment."

"No spruce's here, Miss." Bluey laughed. "Smells great, too. Want me to bring the stepladder in?"

"If you wouldn't mind, Bluey," Dana said. "We're going to start decorating it right away."

When Logan returned to the house he found the women happily engaged in setting up the tree. Already its slender branches were hung with a glittering array of silver, gold, scarlet and green orbs, baubles and ornaments of all kinds, things Ainslie had collected over the years. It came to him he had great affection for the woman his father had married when he was only four. Ainslie had never tried to mother him. Something in him must have held out against it. God knows why. Maybe his soul dwelt with his own mother. The beautiful creature who had died giving him birth. Said to be the image of his father, his father had always told him from the near-empty well of pain, "You have your mother's eyes. Her beautiful, beautiful sapphire eyes. Otherwise, you're a Dangerfield."

Ainslie had come to her marriage knowing she was a kind of rebound, a marriage of convenience, fearing her husband would never truly love her and her stepson would never accept her. Neither had happened. Ainslie was a woman who gave with all her heart, creating her own special place in the Dangerfield family. A position cemented when the children came. Tyler, then Alexandra. Logan remembered he had been ecstatic when his father told him there was going to be an addition to the family. An addition who turned out to be Tyler. He had loved Tyler from the beginning, proud of being big brother, longing for the day when the baby would be old enough for them both to go adventuring in the bush.

Only he and Tyler had been opposites.

And they had both fallen in love with the same woman.

There she was, beautiful, intelligent, gifted Dana, for all of that unassuming, no conceit in any form, full of the social graces. Both Ainslie and Sandra had almost from the start treated her like family. Tyler should have married someone like Dana, he thought grimly. Dana would have understood him, been firm enough, demanding enough to insist Tyler live up to his potential. Tyler had always been capable of so much better. It was their own father who had never understood him, forever holding up Logan as some impossible role model. It was a wonder they had remained as close as they had, Logan thought with deep regret.

Alice, turning, saw him, cried out, "Uncle Logan, come and see the tree. We've only got a few things more to put on. Grandma's little angels. They're all playing instruments."

"And we must be careful how we handle them, darling." Ainslie smiled. "They're quite precious."

"I know." Alice took a bisque porcelain angel very carefully into her hands. "Look at this one. He's playing the violin. I think I'd like to learn a musical instrument."

"That can be arranged." Logan trod across the parqueted floor, covered with a beautiful antique Persian rug, in his riding boots. "How are you, Dana?" he asked suavely. He'd been out since dawn so this was the first time they'd met up. "Sleep well?"

"Like a top," Dana responded just as pleasantly. "You're just in time to place the Star of Bethlehem at the top. None of us can match you for height."

Alice squealed with merriment. "Ladies don't grow *that* tall."

"You should see Bert Bonner's mother," Logan joked. "I practically have to look up to her."

"Really?" Alice asked, wide-eyed.

"Bert says he has to get up on a box to talk to her. Right, Dana, you can pass me the star." Logan put out his hand, catching her fingers briefly as she tried to hand it to him without actually touching him.

Her fingers tingled with electricity.

"Oh, this is so beautiful!" Alice breathed when the glistening silver Star of Bethlehem was in place. "Can we turn on the lights?"

"Go right ahead." Logan stepped down from the ladder, looking up at the tree that almost lofted to the upstairs gallery. Even in daylight the multicoloured lights were a bright illumination, reflecting each sparkling ornament, throwing a kaleidoscope of colour outward in a halo.

"Perhaps a little more tinsel," Dana mused. "That's if we've got any left."

"Plenty of everything in the attic, dear." Ainslie smiled, then inevitably grew sad. "Year after year we've had a tree since the children were babies, but this is the first time we've had it in the hall. I'm glad you came up with that idea, Dana. It makes a lovely change."

Feeling her grief, Logan bent and kissed the side of

his stepmother's cheek. "You're the centre of this house, Ainslie. You've been since the day you came into it."

Ainslie caught her breath. Logan had always had the capacity to surprise her with the perfectly beautiful things he said. For a moment she let her head rest against his shoulder. "It's time to tell you, too, my dear, you've been a wonderful stepson to me. A wonderful brother to my children."

It was an emotional moment that could have turned to tears, but Logan saved it, bowing from the waist, an exaggeratedly formal gesture he managed to pull off with considerable natural grace. "Thank you, Mamma."

Alice came to hold his hand, staring up into his face. "I'm glad I'm here, Uncle Logan. I feel safe."

She, too, seemed on the point of tears. "Your darn right you are!" He picked her up, whirling her around. "I tell you what that tree really needs."

"What?" Alice stared adoringly at him.

"Lots and lots of wonderful presents all around it."

As the countdown to Christmas began, Mara was host to an influx of visitors, younger members of the extended Dangerfield family with their children, friends from all over the Outback popping in and out on private flights, business people from the Outback towns, all wanting to convey their best wishes and enjoy Mara's legendary hospitality at the same time.

The Christmas tree in the entrance hall was now surrounded by a great pile of beautifully wrapped and beribboned presents chosen with care, the papers luxurious, most in the festive colours of Christmas: gleaming silver with ruby, rich gold and emerald, Santa Claus and mistletoe and berries, reindeers, winged angels in flight, all casting their own special glow. The children who came to call found the sight irresistible and Alice for once was in her element playing the small hostess and leader.

Christmas is such a wonderful time of the year it softens everyone's heart and Alice had discovered peace and sunshine in her life. Her "bad moments" when she couldn't cope with the pressures were becoming far less frequent now. There was more understanding in her life, more happy experiences, more encouragement to learn things and build up her own feelings of confidence and inner strength.

Reared in an increasingly unhappy household with her father too little there and her mother not bothering to mask her own unhappiness and frustrations, Alice had not been allowed to grow and blossom. In her new environment she was developing overnight, secure in the love and stability of her family around her. Not that there wasn't the occasional storm, but when it wasn't getting much attention it quickly passed. The thing that most impressed the family was the way Alice was now relating to her own age group, the previous big problem.

"It's not the same as school," she told Dana. "These kids all like me."

Dana took her by the shoulders so she could get Alice's full attention. "So help me they'll *all* like you at school if you're the friendly little person you are here. I'll even go beyond that, Alice, you have the capacity for leadership. It's all up to you, darling, isn't it? You can be anything you want to be. You're clever. You're full of ideas. You're a sensitive little soul. You can afford to take pride in yourself."

"That's right," Alice confirmed with a big smile on her face.

Little trips were organised to entertain, picnics beside the billabongs, where the children looped ropes around the tree and swung out into the water. Even Alice, once a little fearful, tried it, full of life and joy. Her swimming lessons had been progressing and in any case the younger children weren't allowed into the deep.

"You're such a good example to Alice," Sandra told Dana one day as they lazed against cushions watching Alice and the visiting cousins swoop shrieking across the glittering water.

"It's a wonder for her to be within the magic circle." Dana smiled. "Not like school with the other children poking fun at her. Alice loves these children and more wonderfully they love her. Just look at her now."

"Dana, Sandy, watch me, I'm going to let go," she yelled, and fell without a moment's hesitation or fright into the sparkling water where the other children were sporting like small dolphins.

"I do admire the way you handle her." Sandra sighed. "She's changed so much she's almost a different child."

"Well, she had a tough time of it, don't forget. It was a very bad experience for her seeing her parents fighting. She's escaped all that. She feels loved and secure."

"Until the day her mother wants her back," Sandra warned, waving at little Katy. "It's all up to Melinda really. She's the mother, right or wrong."

There was no need to tell Dana. She never stopped worrying about it.

Around this time she also began regular photographic sessions, her mind constantly turning over ideas and possibilities, which, as she moved freely around Mara, seemed to be endless. She had worked a number of times with a well-known travel author and journalist mostly in tropical North Queensland's sugar lands, glorious country, and the wonder of the Great Barrier Reef, which had to be paradise on earth, but nowhere she found so compelling so challenging as the vast Timeless Land. One of the world's harshest environments, it was frighten-

ingly lonely, savage in drought, yet capable of turning
on heart-stopping displays of beauty.

When the time was right, she had seen and photo-
graphed Mara literally covered in flower. Miles and
miles of fragrant flowering annuals that spread in all
directions as far as the eye could see. The wildflowers
were remarkable but so was the prolific bird life, the vast
spinifex plains, the great flat-topped mesas, the crystal-
clear spring-fed pools, the gibber plains that glittered
like a giant mosaic and the magnificent albeit terrifying
sight of the Simpson Desert, the Wild Heart.

More and more she was filled with the invigorating
ambition to capture on camera the very essence of this
mirage-stalked country, to bring it to people who might
never have a chance to see it for themselves. She was
in a unique position to do that with her ties to Mara. It
seemed to her, too, she would like to do her own writing,
convey her own feelings and reactions as she explored
this remote part of the world. Perhaps she could inspire
her readers as she was inspired herself. It gave her lots
to think about. She was grateful, too, for her technical
expertise, though it hadn't come overnight. It was the
result of years of highly specialised training.

Returning one afternoon from one of her treks she
came on a mustering party driving a herd of cleanskins,
cattle as yet unbranded, into one of the holding yards.
Red dust rose in a whirlwind so she parked some little
distance off enjoying the spectacle framed in the dancing
gold-shot blue light. Vivid green butterfly trees grew in
clumps all round the area still heavy in white and mauve
blossom, the earth a bright red ocre, the sky a vivid
cloudless blue. It really was a scene for the cinema
screen, she thought. There were even sound effects.
Cattle lowing, stockmen riding in among them, whips
cracking harmlessly in the air, urging the beasts into the
yard. Every few minutes one would try to make a break

with no success until a young red bull decided it was
high time to leave the mob and head back for the hills.

Through the wall of men came a rider, darting his
horse in and out, nosing the errant animal back into the
enclosure. Both man and horse were lightning quick in
their movements, a pleasure to watch. Dana took up a
position with her Hasselblad, aiming it at the tall lean
cowboy, pearl grey akubra rakishly angled on his dark
head, sitting his bright chestnut horse with easy mastery.

She shot off a half a dozen frames before she became
aware of him riding towards her and holding up his
hand.

"What are you up to?"

She lay the camera down. "Does it require an explanation? I'm taking pictures of you."

"Whatever for?" He seemed genuinely puzzled.

"Because your so damned colourful. You look like
the guy in the old Marlboro commercials, only better,"
she said.

"At least I have the sense not to smoke."

"Pretty well everyone has these days. Why don't you
let me take a few more for my girlfriends," she taunted
him. "Most of them fell in love with you on the strength
of that one photo on my bookcase. You're every
woman's idea of an Outback hero."

"That's me." He smiled with lazy satire. "God, it's
hot!" He took off his hat and ran a hand through his
thick hair. His hands were beautifully shaped. She remembered the feel of them on her body. How she found
their faint callousing and strength so exciting.

"If it's not too personal a question," she asked, "are
we likely to see Phillipa again before Christmas?"

He bent the full force of his brilliant gaze on her.
"Phillipa is past caring about me."

"So that's a no?" With Phillipa, anything was possible. She might have got her second wind.

"More or less." This with a slight edge. "Her parents might turn up. They won't want to cut themselves off from us in any way."

"I guess not," she agreed laconically.

"Where's Alice?" Deliberately, he changed the subject. "The two of you are always together."

"She's having fun with the children. The last time I saw them they were dressing up in the attic. Someone is going to have to put all the stuff they've pulled out of the old trunks away."

"Don't *you* bother about it," he told her. "Now that you're here, why don't we go for a ride?"

For a moment she couldn't think of anything at all to say. They had been well and truly keeping their distance for just on a week now.

"Is there something wrong?" he challenged with the old tantalising mockery.

"Friendly today, are we?"

He gave a brief laugh. "Dana, you're my pain and my delight. Besides, even my iron control doesn't work all the time."

"Then I'd love to." Just for a second she smiled at him. "You'll have to come with me. I haven't got a horse."

"Mine will take both of us."

"You're joking?" Her eyes widened.

"Dana, I mean everything I say. You're a featherweight, that's okay. Or are you frightened of coming up before me?"

His amusement restored her cool. "It works for Alice. I don't know about me."

"So let's try it."

"What about the jeep, my equipment?" She looked around. "It's valuable."

"Don't fret. Who's here to steal it? Cover it with something. Zack can run the jeep back to the house."

She was fiercely tempted even when her wounded feelings were barely healed over.

"Make up your mind," he said, directing a challenging look into her eyes.

"I can't believe I'm doing this." Dana moved to take care of her camera and equipment, covering it with a light rug. Meanwhile Logan rode back a little distance having a short conversation with Zack, his leading hand. She had one last chance to cry off and drive home, only she was too damned excited. This was the sort of man Logan was. All electricity and excitement, and just to prove it while her mind was in arrears, he reached down for her like a stuntman doing tricks and lofted her into the saddle before him. His enveloping arm was an inch from her breasts, his breath fanning her cheek. She scarcely heard the men's applause. She didn't even remember riding out of the camp. They were heading for the crossing fording it at the shallowest point then galloping up the incline to the sheltered valley beyond.

It was a madly heady feeling galloping across the desert flats, the wild bush around them, the wind tearing at her hair, a great flight of budgerigar, the phenomenon of the Outback joyfully joining in the chase, winging in an emerald green and gold V-shaped formation, as though spurring them on. Logan's face was hunkered down over hers, his left arm locked around her upper body, the tips of his fingers pressing into the swelling flesh at the side of her breast. Just to have physical contact was to feel enormously energised. She thought she could have cheerfully ridden to the ends of the earth with him so infinitely spell-binding was his influence over her. Almost unknown to her, her own hands were caressing the length of his bare arm, moving up and down, stroking the light tracery of hair, holding his arm even closer to her so he had to feel her quickening pulses, the primitive throb of her heart. It was almost as though someone had started up a small drum. Over the flats they went until finally they reached the point where their bodies were burning. Not from the heat that rose in waves from the red sun-baked earth, but the heat within. The great all-pervading flames neither of them could put out. This was part of the sorcery of love, the recklessness, the anguish, the ferocious need for physical fulfilment.

Finally, Logan rode down on a spring-fed pool, clear cool water oozing up from the sandy bed, the pool lined by long reeds the area totally surrounded by stands of desert oaks. He dismounted swiftly, seized Dana, pulled her from the saddle and into his waiting arms. He was mad for her, even dangerous, he thought. In truth he was trying to get a hold on himself, hating the sense of going out of control, but he wanted this woman too much. He could never have foreseen how terribly he would want her.

Forgetful of his strength, he almost lifted her off her feet to kiss her, pushing her head back into his shoulder, covering her mouth passionately as if kissing her was as necessary to him as the air he breathed or the precious water without which a man would die. He kissed her over and over as if this was his one and only chance, his hand moving, moving, deeply massaging her spine, moulding her body ever closer. Her mouth tasted of apricots, her skin smelled like wildflowers after rain. He knew she was breathless, panting in his arms, but she wasn't struggling away. The more he wanted, the more her body gave. He plunged his hand into the open neck of her soft shirt, breaking a button, but anything to get to her exquisite naked breast. Now he understood fully how that one woman could change a man's life. He didn't want an affair. An affair would be wrong. He wanted this woman to love all the days of his life. He wanted to be free of the torment. He wasn't good at giving up the things he wanted.

She hadn't been wearing her hair loose but the wind had whipped it free of its ribbon. Now he grasped a handful of this beautiful long hair he loved, turning her head to the side so he could kiss her lovely neck. She was quivering in his arms. Burying her face against his shoulder, moaning a little as though her heart was breaking.

He drew a breath so sharp it hurt his ribs. "Let me love you," he urged. "I would never force you. But let me love you."

Her eyes were so dark yet at the centre was a leaping flame. She began to laugh, a soft wild little sound, no mirth in it but a kind of acknowledged abandonment. "We said we wouldn't."

"I know." His face was full of urgent hungers, a desire that raged. "You want it though, Dana, don't you?"

Want? She was ravenous. She let her head fall back, stretching her throat. "Ah…*yes!*" She wasn't a woman who had ever expected to be totally dominated by a man yet nonetheless she was. Logan consumed her. It was that simple.

CHAPTER TEN

THREE days before Christmas the peace of the household was shattered when Melinda flew in unannounced and alone. Logan, who saw the four-seater Cessna fly in, doubled back to the landing strip in the four-wheel drive, his eyes focused on the charter flight that was just coming in to land. He felt absolutely no warning. Visitors had been flying in and out for most of December. Usually, though, they always rang ahead to say they were coming. He was familiar with the charter plane. It was one of Westaway's. Ray Westaway was a good friend. It was probably Ray come to say hello and pay his respects to Ainslie. By the time he drove the vehicle to the strip, the plane had landed and the pilot was on the strip, handing down a young woman.

Melinda.

Dismay welled up in him, a fierce sense of protectiveness for his family, Alice in particular. Whatever Melinda was doing here it could only spell trouble. A harsh judgement to some but he knew her too well.

The pilot came towards him, smiling like he was among friends, carrying his passenger's two pieces of luggage. "Hi, there, Mr. Dangerfield. One passenger delivered safely." He turned to include the very pretty blonde who was showing for the first time an unexpected uneasiness? Wariness? Whatever. Dangerfield wasn't smiling. To the pilot's mind he looked positively formidable. This was his reputation anyway. A powerful man who had stepped very neatly into his father's shoes. And he was angry. Quite angry. He had never seen such a blaze in a man's eyes before.

A few minutes later the pilot flew off, feeling molli-
fied Dangerfield had greeted him pleasantly, giving him
a message to convey to his boss. He remembered now
they were good friends.

On the ground, Logan settled Melinda in the front
passenger seat then went around to the other side, opening up the door and climbing behind the wheel. "You're
full of surprises, Melinda," he said, trying to view the
arrival calmly. "I understood you were enjoying yourself in London?"

Melinda touch a hand to her short, pretty hair. She
was doing it a new way and she looked older and more
sophisticated than he had ever seen her. "Max hates the
cold. He has great friends in Sydney. We're staying with
them."

"So it's serious, then, with Max?" What exactly had
Tyler meant in his wife's life? he thought with a heavy
heart, asking, "What's Max's other name?"

"He's the man I'm probably going to marry,"
Melinda evaded. "It doesn't matter his name."

"I'm afraid it does, Melinda, as you're Alice's
mother."

"I've learned to keep a few things to myself," she
said, "for the time being anyway."

"You could have let us know you were coming."

"Don't be awkward, Logan. It was a spur-of-the-
moment thing. I wanted to give you all a big surprise."

"Then I have to say I find your idea of a big surprise
pretty bizarre. You can't expect us to feel overjoyed
about it."

"Well, it was never your way, was it?" Melinda gave
him her kittenish triangular smile.

They were even more shocked at the house. The moment Melinda set foot in the entrance hall exclaiming at
the Christmas tree, the pervading tranquillity seemed to
fly out the door.

"Melinda!" Ainslie tried her level best for courtesy and calm. "This is indeed a surprise. We didn't expect you back so soon."

"Only a flying visit. A week or two to miss the Winter. "Dana!" Melinda held out her arms as Dana for a few moments transfixed started down the stairs. "My very *favourite* cousin."

"Good God, Melinda," Dana responded in a heartfelt groan. "Couldn't you have let us know you were coming?"

"Why, Dee. Don't you like surprising people? I'm here with Max, actually. We're staying with friends of his, right on the Harbour. An absolute mansion. The Goddards. You must have heard of them." She named a well-known racing family then stopped abruptly as though she had given away too much. "I slipped away for a time. I hope you don't mind, but I have a few things to straighten out."

"Of course," Ainslie answered, still shocked. "You're staying overnight surely?"

"I'd like that." Melinda smiled. "I can't be away from Max's side for any longer than that. And Alice, where is she?"

Logan couldn't help the cynical laugh that broke from him. "I was wondering when you were going to mention your daughter." He gestured towards the formal drawing room. "Let's go in and sit down, shall we?" He turned his head briefly to speak to Dana. "Would you mind finding Alice, please, Dana. You could prepare her by telling her her mother is here."

Dana sprang into action almost running through the house. What did Melinda's sudden appearance mean? Was it possible Melinda was becoming more human? Did she intend to resume her God-given role and take Alice back with her? If so, they would miss Alice dreadfully. And what of Alice's feelings? And who was this

Max? How serious was the relationship? Was he the sort of man who would be prepared to love another man's child? And *Jimmy!* Had he really meant so little to Melinda she had already put him out of her life?

She came bursting out of the house, finding Alice sitting beside Retta on the grass. They were spreading out drawings, things Alice had completed with Retta acting as teacher. Retta was a very talented artist, both in the traditional aboriginal way and the Western culture. She had already shown Alice an easy way to draw animals.

"There you are!" Dana breathed.

They both turned at the tight, constricted sound in Dana's normally warm melodious tones.

"I've got a good little pupil here." Retta smiled, then with her enviable sensitivity picked up on Dana's agitated feelings. "Everything okay, Miss Dana?"

Pray God it was. "Yes, fine, Retta." Dana tried for a smile that didn't quite come off. "Thank you so much for looking after Alice, but she has to come into the house now."

"Ah, Dana, I'm having a nice time," Alice complained.

"Yes, I know you are, darling, but something has happened. I want to tell you all about it."

"You're not upset about it, are you?" Alice rose immediately to her feet, staring into Dana's face.

"No, dear." Dana turned to address Retta who was standing quietly nearby. "Perhaps you could collect the drawings, Retta. I'd love to see them later."

"No trouble. Go along now, Alice. We can take a walk together later."

Inside the house, Dana drew Alice into the kitchen storeroom. "Listen, darling, a very big surprise. Mummy is here. She wants to see you."

For answer, Alice reached out, picked up a small can of baked beans and threw it violently against the wall.

"If this means I have to go back with her I'm not coming."

"Alice," Dana came close to wailing, taking the child into her arms. "This is *Mummy*. She's been missing you."

"Well, I haven't been missing her." Alice frowned ferociously, twisting away. "I don't want her anymore, Dana. I like things the way they are."

"But will you always, Alice," she pleaded. "Your mother has hurt you, but give her a chance. She's come all this way out here to make amends."

"You take care of me, Dana," Alice said, her light brown head dropping. "Mummy is mean to me. She doesn't like me. She doesn't want me around."

"Alice, please, why don't you let her tell you how sorry she is? Please give her another chance. Mummy was hurt, too."

Alice looked up into Dana's eyes. "You really want this, Dana. You're not punishing me?"

Dana almost reeled back in shock. "Punishing you. Lord, sweetheart, would I ever do that? Would I ever do anything to make you unhappy?"

"Daddy said you didn't know about Mummy."

"Daddy had his own problems. Mummy and I grew up together. We've been together all our lives."

"And what does Uncle Logan and Grandma say?" Alice looked her straight in the eye.

"We're all trying to understand our feelings, darling. Maybe we all can't be together nice and friendly like your cousins and the children, but we have to learn how to cope with what's going on in our lives. You're growing up now, Alice. You're a serious little person. I only want you to greet your mother and listen to what she has to say. Parents must be treated with dignity and respect."

"Kids have to be treated with respect, too," Alice

burst out, giving vent to all her pent-up feelings of hurt and rejection.

"You should be happy Mummy's here," Dana said sorrowfully.

"Well, I'm not." Alice reached out and grasped Dana's hand. "This is important to you, Dana, isn't it?"

"Important to you, too, darling." Dana squeezed her small hand, praying and praying Melinda would come into her own and express loving maternal feelings. She had changed a good deal in appearance. Indeed she was looking stunning. With the grace of God she would make up for the hurt she had inflicted on her child.

When they went into the drawing room, Melinda, sitting alone on a Victorian settee, jumped up, a radiant smile on her face. "Alice, sweetie, don't you look well. The prettiest I've ever seen you. Come to Mummy and give me a great big hug."

Alice hesitated a moment, turned and looked at Dana, then walked towards her mother.

"Hello, Mummy," she said composedly. "Didn't you like London?"

"I loved it! I can't wait to go back." Melinda bent over Alice and kissed the cheek her daughter presented. "This is what is called a flying visit."

"Why?" Alice asked.

"Why what?"

"Why did you come?" Alice asked. "It's a long trip just to see me."

"That's right, and I am a little tired. Aren't you pleased to see me?" Melinda's blue eyes looked hurt.

"You look very pretty," Alice commented.

Melinda brightened. "Well, I know I can never be a genuine beauty like Dee but I can turn a few heads. Why don't you come up to my room while I have a little rest? We can talk. Is that all right, Ainslie?" Melinda turned her blond head.

"Of course, Melinda," Ainslie answered quietly. "I'm hoping when you're feeling refreshed you can tell us your plans."

"Oh, I will." Melinda took hold of Alice's hand. "I've lots to catch up on with my daughter."

"Come with us, Dana," Alice begged.

"Not now, Alice." Melinda gave a little smile. "I know you love Dana, but I'm hoping you can spare a little time for your mother."

"Dear God!" Logan said slowly and deliberately after they had gone. "What does all this mean?"

"I couldn't bear to lose Alice now," Ainslie said piteously. "To take her away to another country! Don't grandparents lose out."

"Who said anything about her wanting to take Alice away?" Logan asked, a vertical frown between his black brows. "It's a good thing Sandy isn't here or we could have a fight on our hands."

"Give her a chance, Logan," Dana implored.

"You *want* her to take Alice?"

"No, no." Dana slumped dejectedly into an armchair. "But she is Alice's mother."

"Of course she is," Ainslie agreed wretchedly. "If only she was a real mother. A real person. I don't think she's changed."

Dinner was a quiet meal with a kind of unbearable tension beneath the superficial conversation. Alice had been allowed to stay up, now she sat beside her mother, wrapped in a blanket of silence.

"Everything all right, my little love?" Ainslie asked, her pale face showing her anxiety. "You're not eating."

"I have a headache, Grandma," Alice said quietly.

"Naturally she's wanting me to stay on," Melinda said.

"I imagine she might, as you're her mother," Logan

clipped off. It was driving him wild Melinda just sitting there saying nothing. He had the dismal feeling she was toying with them, playing some preconceived game.

Alice spoke again. "I don't care if Mummy goes." From the expression on her face there could be no doubt she meant it.

"That's not very nice, sweetie," Melinda said.

"It's what I want," Alice exclaimed.

Melinda reached for her wineglass and picked it up. "I can see you've all been doing your best to turn my child against me," she said acidly.

Dana looked directly at her cousin with angry eyes, then she pushed back her chair and stood up. "If you have a headache, Alice, why don't I take you up to your room?"

"I want her to stay," Melinda said.

"I think not." Logan gestured to Dana to go. "This conversation is obviously for the grown-ups."

In her bedroom Alice slumped down dejectedly on the bed. "I belong to Mummy. Is that right, Dana?"

"Pretty well, darling, until you're older."

"So she can take me at any time?"

Yes, Dana thought. "If you want that, darling."

"Well, I don't." There was rebellion in Alice's voice. "I want to stay here. I don't want to go away. I would miss you terribly. I would miss Grandma and Uncle Logan and Sandy. I would miss all the kids when they come to visit. I'd miss Mrs. Buchan. Retta, too. She's so sweet to me. Mara is a wonderful happy place."

This was a dilemma and it was tearing at Dana's heartstrings. "Don't you think you could be happy with Mummy?"

"Not the way I want to be," Alice said slowly.

"Did Mummy say she was going to take you?" Dana didn't like to question Alice too closely but they had to know.

"She was talking mostly about you," Alice surprised her by saying.

"Me?"

"You and Uncle Logan." Alice nodded her head. "She asked how you were getting on."

"And what did you say?"

"I said Uncle Logan loves you and you love him. I can feel it deep inside." Alice clasped her small hands together and pressed them to her heart. "I've been praying you'd get married then I could be your child."

"Oh, Alice." Dana sat down on the bed and caught the little girl to her. "Oh, Alice," she moaned, "this is so very very hard for all of us. I'm your godmother. I'll always be your godmother. I'll always be there for you."

"I'm afraid," Alice said.

It took Dana close on half an hour to settle the child for bed, so when she returned downstairs she found the family had adjourned to the library.

"Alice is asleep at last," she said as she walked into the room, acutely aware of the tension that clouded the atmosphere.

"You've quite taken her over, haven't you, Dee?" Melinda said, not troubling to hide her disdain.

"You didn't seem too concerned about doing the job," Logan reminded her very abruptly. "You've obviously come to tell us of your intentions, so we'd appreciate it if you would. Alice has had a very disruptive life. She's only now settling down."

"Why this endless talk of Alice?" Melinda fumed. "She's had a pretty good life. Anyone would think she was suffering some abuse."

Logan stared at her from his position behind the massive mahogany desk. Behind him, above the mantelpiece hung a portrait of his grandfather, a sternly handsome man with a look of power and achievement. It was obvious they were cut from the same cloth. "Ever heard of emotional deprivation," he said.

"It seems to me I know more about it than you do," Melinda retorted. "I'm the original deprived child."

"That's right, the never-ending story," Dana burst out. "Deprived of your parents certainly, Melinda, but not of plenty of love and attention. You've never been gracious enough to acknowledge that. Anyway I would have thought your own emotional deprivation would have made you more understanding. More determined to see Alice would have a good life."

"It's a great relief then, isn't it, she's an heiress," Melinda countered. "Which brings me to my proposition," she went on calmly. "I'm willing to sign papers relating to *your* guardianship of Alice, Logan, if that's what you all want. You don't seem to be able to hide it. There is, however, a price."

"Really?" Logan's voice was marvellously ironical. "How did I know that was coming."

Melinda flushed and stood up abruptly, beginning to pace the far end of the spacious room. A pretty, petite figure in a short, gold-embroidered navy dress. "Max is a wealthy man, but I have no intention of being dependent on him like I was on Jimmy."

"You have a not considerable inheritance from my son," Ainslie pointed out bleakly, glad Sandra wasn't there to hear this.

"I want more," Melinda said flatly. "A lot more. You've got it."

"What sort of money are we talking about here?" Logan demanded, his handsome mouth thinning.

"Another five million," Melinda said as though that was more than fair. "It doesn't seem much for a child and you Dangerfields always figure in the Rich List."

She didn't have long to wait for Logan's answer. "I'm

terribly sorry, Melinda," he said very quietly, "but it's not on."

"Logan!" Ainslie stared at her stepson as if to measure the wisdom of his words. What was money compared to the happiness and well-being of her granddaughter?

"See, Ainslie agrees!" Melinda turned on him in triumph. "What about you, Dana? You know how important your opinion is to Logan," she said, with sly meaning.

"I'm not believing this," Dana said, a slight betraying tremor in her voice. "Are you saying you're prepared to *sell* your child?"

Melinda shrugged. "Well, I'd certainly like to see her from time to time. Don't look so damned righteous. You've always told me I'm a poor mother."

"Even so, I'm not handing over another penny," Logan cut across them, rising to his daunting six-three. "So what are the other options, Melinda?" he asked, watching her pretty kitten face suddenly look pinched.

"I'll collect her after Christmas. You won't have her, I'll see to that."

"And Max is in agreement with all this?" Logan looked suave.

"Anything I do is fine with Max," Melinda said shortly. "He's madly in love with me."

"Poor devil! He's happy to take on a ready-made child, is he?" Logan continued.

"He certainly is!" Melinda huffed.

"Then why not take her now before Christmas?" Logan suggested, quite reasonably. "I see no reason to wait. You're Alice's mother. No one can deny that. You want her. Well and good. You can't expect us to keep looking after her. I say take her tomorrow. We have all her clothes ready."

For the first time Melinda appeared aghast and she

wasn't the only one. Ainslie covered her face with her hands and Dana sprang up, velvety brown eyes flashing fire. "You can't mean this, Logan. You can't," she cried, knowing Logan had a ruthless streak.

"Indeed I do," he said harshly. "I won't be black-mailed."

"It's Alice's whole life that's at stake." She went closer to him, caught hold of his arm.

"I thought you were the one who was telling us all to give Melinda a chance." He looked down at her. "Something miraculous was to happen and she'd turn over a new leaf."

"Please, Logan," she begged. "Won't you consider it? She can have what money Jimmy left me. I haven't touched it."

"You're not seeing this clearly, Dana," he told her, his blue eyes cold. "I'm the head of this household and I say, *no*. Melinda has received more than enough and I have no intention of getting into a legal battle. If she's going to marry this Max and he is quite happy about assuming the responsibilities of a stepfather, I say Melinda should cut all the anguish short and take Alice now."

"Excuse me, dear. I'm going to bed," Ainslie said, rising a little unsteadily to her feet. "You must do as you think best."

"Let me take you up." Logan moved swiftly to support his stepmother. "I'm sure you and Dana have things to say to each other, Melinda," he threw over his shoulder. "I won't be long."

Both young women were silent until long after the sounds of footsteps had died away, then Melinda launched into a plea, a well-remembered febrile look in her light blue eyes. "Talk to him. Convince him this is the best way to do it."

"What makes you think I could possibly sway Logan," Dana demanded. "He's a law unto himself."

"Come on, Dee." Melinda flashed her a look. "You two have something going, haven't you? You've always been in love with him only you were too stupid to see it."

Dana ignored that. "I'm telling you, once Logan has made up his mind, no one on earth could change it for him."

"But you must *try,*" Melinda insisted with extreme intensity. "Invite him into your bed, that's if you haven't done it already. I bet he's one hell of a lover, too. All that fire! But underneath, he's cruel. He professed to love Alice yet he's prepared to let her go."

Dana, too, was unprepared for his reaction. "What did you expect him to do?" she said wretchedly. "Pay up just like that. Who could ever trust you anyway?"

"You can trust me *easily,*" Melinda maintained.

"How's that? You've been a liar all your life. You've lied about me."

"And enjoyed it," Melinda clipped off, crisply decisive.

"Why would you want to hurt me, Melinda? Hurt Jimmy's memory?" Dana asked very seriously.

"I've buried Jimmy," Melinda flashed back. "He was unfaithful to me God knows how many times. If you weren't one of his women it was only because his feeling for you was all tenderness. Dear sweet Dana, the embodiment of all that is good."

"So why did you write to Logan telling him Jimmy and I had an affair?" Dana asked heavily.

"Oh, jealousy I suppose," Melinda cried in exasperation. "What kind of an idiot are you? I've always been jealous of you. Even your friends told you that. Why should you have a man crazy about you? I never had."

"What about this Max?" Dana rushed in, frowning.

"What's the big secret about his last name? Does he even *exist?*"

"It's Max De Winter, if you must know," Melinda joked. Then, "No, it's Max Ferguson. No need to tell Logan, I don't want him checking up on me. Max is a lot older than I am, as I told you, but he's an impressive-looking man and he can give me the life I've always wanted."

"And he wants a child?" Dana was starting to wonder.

"Exactly. A ready-made one. He won't want me to fall pregnant. We'll be doing a lot of travelling together. Entertaining. He has a lot of business interests across the Atlantic and here. I could see Alice when we're in the country."

"Gee, that's big of you." Dana shook her head sadly. "I just don't understand you, Melly."

"When did you ever?" Melinda retaliated, sweeping out of the room and up the staircase to her bedroom, where she locked it.

Dam all the Dangerfields to hell! Especially Logan.

Dana waited quite a while for Logan to return. She stood by the window looking sightlessly out over the moonlit garden, desperately trying to keep herself together. Could Logan really bring himself to pass Alice over at this time? At Christmas, when Alice was the happiest she had ever been?

She could understand his anger at Melinda's demands for money. A great fortune to most people but not people like the Dangerfields, the establishment since pioneering days. She'd had to face, much as she regretted it, Melinda would never become the person she had hoped. Melinda was a bitter disappointment, with little capacity for parenthood. So why then, if she didn't get the money, was she going to take Alice? Because the current pivotal person in her life, Max, wanted it? Would a middle-aged businessman who travelled extensively want a small child? Was Alice to be shunted to a boarding school? Why didn't Logan just pay the money? Let her have it. Could he see the loss of her grandchild would shatter Ainslie's life? Let alone hers. Hadn't she sworn to Alice she would never abandon her?

By the time Logan did return, Dana, for all her efforts, had worked herself into an emotional state. It showed in the line of her body, her flushed skin and the glitter in her dark eyes.

"We won't stop here," Logan said in his command-ing way, taking her arm and ushering her out onto the colonnaded terrace. "Let's get away from the house. I take it Melinda has gone up to bed?"

"Yes." Her response was brittle but it was the best she could do. "She's beside herself her little scheme mightn't work."

He tried to restrain the abrasiveness that was in him but failed. "So you've finally got your eyes open?"

That stung her. "I'm not like you, Logan, I'm sorry," she answered in a jagged voice. "You have a rare talent for being able to categorise people on sight. I like to give them a chance."

"Well, you must be feeling you've made one hell of a mistake tonight." He tossed her a tight smile. "Your cousin is what's known as a gold digger."

"It certainly looks like it. But she's dealing with the wrong person, isn't she? The toughest negotiator for miles."

"I wouldn't last long if I weren't and I've had a lot more exposure than you to the underside of human na-ture. Let's walk."

"Anything you say, Logan." She meant to mock him, instead it echoed the pain in her heart. She let him lead her down the short flight of steps onto the circular drive with the lights from the house playing over the three-tier fountain. "Is Ainslie all right?" she asked, looking up into his face. A handsome face. A proud face. "It worries me to see her so upset."

"You surprise me, Dana." He used the sleek tone she knew so well. "Don't you think I can look after my stepmother?"

"I'm certain you *mean* to."

"You can't expect me to adopt your sweet girlish ways. Ainslie's willing to let me handle this situation. Unlike *you.*"

She tried unsuccessfully to hold on to her temper. "That's really weird. Ainslie must know all about your ruthless streak."

"Oddly she regards me as the perfect stepson. What's so ruthless about what I'm doing, anyway?" he countered.

They had begun walking, now she stopped in the semi-darkness of the trees and faced him. "You're prepared to let Alice go?"

"You mean I'm not doing what Melinda is asking," he corrected, his voice hard.

"I can't bear to think about it." Dana began to move on, agitation racing through her blood. How could she love Logan when he tied her in knots?

He caught her up easily, whirling her around. "It might pay you to use your mind and not your emotions. You're tearing yourself to pieces. That's not a man's way."

"Hell no!" She reacted with unconcealed hostility, pushing against his strong hands but he only tightened his grip on her. "Why would the all powerful cattle baron accept blackmail?"

"It's not going to come to that."

"Why? What are you going to do to stop it?" Even

when they were arguing her pulses were all aglitter, her heartbeats racing.

"I'm going to call Melinda's bluff. Pulling stunts doesn't sit well with me and that's what's she's doing. It would be great if it could come off. An extra five million to get on with her life." He stared down into her face, shifting her a little so she was caught in the full moon's copper radiance. "You don't really think she wants Alice, do you, or are you still wallowing in all those cousinly marshmallow feelings?"

"You hate women, don't you?" she accused him.

He seemed amused. "Only one of you can drive me nuts and I'm looking at her."

She tried desperately to interpret every nuance in his voice. "I'm scared of what she'll do, Logan. Can't you understand that?"

"Of course I can." He released one hand to cup her nape. "You've had too much trouble dealing with your cousin. Now you have to leave her to me. Are you prepared to do that?"

"I don't have much choice." She moved her head against his hand, unable to resist the basic sensual pleasure.

"No, you don't," he agreed. "But you could have some faith. While you've been thinking of ways to kill me, I've been calling in a few favours."

That would explain his time away. "Good heavens!" Dana stared up at him in surprise. "You should be running the country."

"No thanks, but we now have the lowdown on Max. Max Ferguson is his name. Melinda let slip she was staying with the Goddards. I don't know them personally, but I have plenty of connections who do. One's Eve Goddard's brother."

Frantically she considered the ramifications. "Could this damage Melinda?"

He tilted her chin. "Do you care?"

"I can't help caring, Logan. It's the way I am."

"Sure." His voice softened. "Anyway, Max is over fifty. He already has a grown up family."

Dana's eyes widened. "You can't mean he's married?" She felt shocked.

"Not exactly. He's divorced."

"Good grief!" She had to steady herself against him and he drew her right into his arms. "The word is out and it's all very confidential, Max would be highly unlikely to want to start another family. He has one and he's a very busy man. The whisper is Melinda is part of a package. She's young, she's blond. Max has always preferred blondes, and she has a nice little nest egg of her own."

"Most people would call it a lot. Does your friend know if he means to marry her?" Dana asked, wondering if Melinda had made yet another mistake.

"Apparently she's just what Max needs in his life."

"And Mrs. Goddard won't say a word?"

Logan shook his head. "She swears she won't mention the phone call to another soul. I don't know that I can see her doing that in the fullness of time but by then Melinda and Max should be out of the country."

"Without Alice?"

"That's what we're counting on," Logan said a little grimly.

"I know you keep a perfect picture of motherhood in your head, but you'll have to accept all Melinda thinks about is herself."

"So she was lying?"

"Isn't it something she does all the time?" He took a skein of her hair and twisted it around his arm.

"One of her lies was pretty effective with you."

"Especially when everyone else was saying the same thing."

Her eyes were sad. "You're going to break my heart, Logan, if you don't believe me."

She looked so perfect, a moon maiden, with her lustrous skin and long gilded hair. Her skin was warm to the touch, almost feverish like below the surface there were sparks in her blood. It drove him to straining her to him, the slender, almost fragile body he couldn't get enough of.

"Could I?" he asked.

"You know the answer to that."

"I thought it was my heart on the line?" His voice was deep, caressing, heavy with desire. As his dark head came down, Dana lowered her eyes, feeling the exquisite crush of his mouth over hers, the fierce strength of his arms that excited her so intensely. She knew he was in love with her, perhaps in his heart of hearts *loved* her, but she had gotten to the point where she believed there could be no future for them if she couldn't have Logan's trust.

Dana was never to forget the early part of the next morning. Despite Logan's assurances, his insistence that calling Melinda's bluff would save the day, Melinda was full of qualms. Melinda was a parent who didn't hesitate to project her own conflicts on her child. She had even done her best to cause Dana harm. At some deep psychological level Melinda was a person full of resentments and frustrations. The family was trying desperately to recover from Jimmy's death yet Melinda seemed hellbent on causing them more pain with her actions. It all added up to the fact Melinda was a loose cannon.

When Dana very quietly entered Alice's room to check that the little girl was all right, instead of a sleeping child she encountered an empty bed. Already suffused with anxieties she checked the bathroom, the veranda outside Alice's room. No sign of her. Next she hurried down to Melinda's room, tapped on it briefly, then finding the door unlocked pushed it open and went in. It was still early. Not quite seven o'clock. She remembered now Melinda hated being woken out of a sleep but her concerns about Alice were making her jumpy.

Melinda had her narrow back to her, curled up in sleep, but there was no Alice beside her.

"Melinda?" Dana didn't hesitate to call urgently. "Wake up."

"What?" Melinda stirred, muttering very crossly. She turned on her back, her blond curls a halo around her small face, one strap of her luxurious nightgown falling off her white shoulder. "What the heck is going on, Dee? Are you throwing me out or what?"

"I can't find Alice," Dana answered, holding her hands together tightly.

"Great!" Melinda groaned. "She'll be around some place."

"She should be in her bed," Dana said worriedly.

"Kids get up early. You know that. What's the matter with you? You're like some poor old mother hen."

"What did you say to her, Melly?" Dana advanced on the bed, such a fire in her eyes Melinda sat up straight.

"Nothing!" Melinda snapped.

"You didn't tell her you wanted to take her back to Sydney with you?"

"It's Logan who decided she has to go," Melinda reminded her angrily. "Always set himself up as the wonderful uncle, too. Now he can't wait to get rid of her."

Dana decided to strike while the iron was hot. "Then you've accepted he won't pay up?"

"You're sure of it, too?" Melinda searched her cousin's face. Dana would never lie to her.

"You know Logan, Melly," Dana said, as if that were sufficient explanation. "He's as hard as nails."

Melinda nodded, biting her lip. "Like that Getty? Remember when he wouldn't pay up for his grandson?"

"That's right, so you might as well forget your little scheme. We'll have Alice ready for you by the time you leave."

"Oh, God." Melinda closed her eyes tightly then she stripped back the bedclothes and stood up, a pocket venus in her peach satin nightdress. She had lost quite a bit of weight and she looked little more than the young girl Dana remembered. "You have to wonder about some people," she said, reaching for her matching robe and putting it on. "I thought you loved Alice?"

"I do." Dana nodded, in one way not wanting to do this but she had no choice. "But you're Alice's mother. We must all focus on that."

"But damn it all, I don't want her!" Frustration distorted Melinda's voice. "I *can't* want her. Max knows I have a daughter who lives with her grandmother. I explained Alice is quite difficult and needs special attention. He understands that, but he doesn't want or need a small child to disrupt his world."

Dana forced her voice to remain even. "Let me get this straight. You've come out here trying to extort money? Is that it?"

"Bunkum. It's justice, Dee. Haven't you ever heard of justice? Alice is the heiress not me."

"And Max is prepared to marry you only if Alice remains with her family?"

"Can you blame him," Melinda retorted, as if Dana was stating the obvious.

"I expect he has a family of his own tucked away some place?" Dana said grimly. "Are you sure he's not married?"

Melinda stood stock-still, suddenly uneasy. "He's *divorced.*"

"I guess Logan could talk to him," Dana suggested. "Establish you're not without family."

Evidently that was the last thing Melinda wanted. "Leave Logan out of this," she cried. "I don't want him interfering in my affairs."

"Then I suggest you come clean with your intentions, Melly," Dana said shortly. "Get it over. He'll be as mad as hell but it probably won't go any further. Alice has to have stability in her life. Make Logan her legal guardian. You need have no fears. He'll look after her and he won't deny you access to your own child."

Melinda began to drum her fingers on a small marquetry table. "You're absolutely sure I couldn't break him down?" She glanced at Dana, who shrugged.

"*Convinced.* Logan means what he says. I should have known but it shocked me nevertheless." Hurriedly she turned to the door. "I'll get back to you, Melly. I'm going downstairs. With any luck Alice might be with Mrs. Buchan eating breakfast."

Mrs. Buchan was surprised. "I haven't laid eyes on her, Dana. She doesn't come downstairs until around eight o'clock, as you know." She stepped closer, speaking in a confidential murmur. "You don't think she could be hiding? She's done it before. In the old days when life got too much for her."

"*Hiding?*" Given that Alice was very upset it was more than likely. But where? There were a million wild acres out there. Even the house was huge. "Where's Mr. Dangerfield?" she asked, feeling she needed Logan beside her.

Mrs. Buchan considered. "I fed him breakfast at six. He wanted to be at the Four Mile when the men came in. Other than that I can't say."

"We'll have to search the house from top to bottom,"

Dana said. "Someone has to go for Logan. Alice could have headed out into the bush."

The search began in earnest and a short time after Logan strode through the front door. "Why didn't I consider this is what she might do?" he said, his eyes flashing. "Alice has always been full of action."

"You don't think she's in danger?" Dana's pale face was showing her anxiety.

"I'll bet my riding boots she's just hiding out." Logan went to her, pulled her into his arms, let her head rest against him as her support.

"My, isn't that a touching scene!" Melinda called, coming daintily down the stairs. "I always knew you two would get together at some point."

"So that made you tell all your lies," Logan confronted bluntly.

"Well, you did get hooked for a time." Melinda looked completely undisturbed. "Jimmy may have hankered after Dee but even for him she was the princess in the tower. You know, *inaccessible.*"

"But you decided to hang it on him all the same." Logan shook his head, feeling a vast shame and anger. In doubting Dana he deserved to lose her.

"Jimmy ripped my heart out with his infidelities," Melinda retorted. "I owe him nothing. Dana and I have been together since childhood. I love her, I guess. I don't really mind hurting her, either, from time to time. And while you're all knocking yourselves out searching for Alice as though no one else matters, I should tell you she's given to this sort of behaviour. Just her way of looking for attention. I'd advise you to get on with what you're doing and the little devil will come home. She'll be hiding out until she figures it's safe."

"Safe?" Dana asked the question, sounding appalled.

"Until I'm gone," Melinda explained. "The moment

she hears the plane take off she'll come out of her hiding place.''

"Very likely," Logan agreed, his voice quiet. "But surely you feel some anxiety?"

"Do you?" Melinda countered. "That child's a Dangerfield. I've said it all along."

Melinda flew out at ten o'clock sharp, convinced there was no remote cause for worry and that's exactly how it turned out, though the search continued unabated, spreading out into the bush. It was Dana who found her, given a clue by one of the drawings Alice had made with Retta the day before. It was a picture of the Dangerfield stone chapel, an excellent drawing for a child, showing its Gothic features and the tall spire. Even an attempt had been made at drawing the intricate design on the beautiful wrought-iron gates that enclosed the grounds. A church. A chapel. Historically, a safe haven.

Alice was nowhere to be seen inside but when Dana called her name, trying to communicate all the love and protectiveness that was in her, Alice suddenly emerged from behind the altar, rising a little stiffly from her cramped position.

"It's all right, I'm here. Were you worried?" She stared at Dana with big over-bright eyes.

"Oh, darling, you mustn't do that again," Dana said when they were through hugging one another. "We're only looking to do what's best for you."

"Not if you mean to send me back with Mummy," Alice maintained stubbornly. "If you hadn't found me I'd probably have stayed here until I heard the plane."

"But you understand, don't you, Grandma has suffered enough grief? She's not young anymore. We mustn't worry her."

"I'm sorry." Alice hung her head, shrinking from the vision of her grandmother's sad face. "I love Grandma,

I love you all. I even love Mummy if she'll only leave me alone.''

"We must go back to the house," Dana said decisively, holding out her hand.

"I'm not," Alice cried passionately, backing away. "Mummy does what she likes. She doesn't care how anyone feels."

"She's not taking you back to Sydney, Alice, I promise."

"Are you sure?" Alice watched Dana closely.

"I'm certain. I probably shouldn't be discussing this with you now but it might put your mind to rest. Mummy has decided Uncle Logan can be your legal guardian. You'll be able to see Mummy anytime you like but you'll be living here." Where you belong, Dana thought.

Alice held out her hand, obviously imitating her Uncle Logan. "Will we shake on that."

"I'm pleased to." They shook hands. "Can we go up to the house now?" Dana asked. "I want everyone to know you're safe."

"I bet Uncle Logan wasn't worried." Alice grinned.

"He knows all about your bolting."

"What did Mummy say?" Alice gave her an intense stare.

"Mummy is worried, like the rest of us. Even Uncle Logan is under some strain. You could have wandered off into the wild."

"No way!" Alice snapped off. "I could have got lost."

Dana went to take the little girl's hand, anxious to return to the house, but Alice escaped, entering a pew and ramming her small frame into the corner. "As soon as I hear the plane." Her voice was still wary. "You can go and whisper to Grandma I'm all right, if you like."

Dana sighed, lifted her wrist and stared down at her watch. There wasn't much longer to go before Melinda's flight. She moved into the pew, reached for Alice, who fell sideways into her lap.

On Christmas another contingent of Dangerfield relatives arrived to spend Christmas Day and Boxing Day on the station. It was a yearly ritual with different members of the extended family taking turns. This year because Alice was in residence, younger members had been invited to bring their small children to join in all the fun.

Another Dangerfield ritual was the Christmas Eve party. Not only for the family, but for everyone on the station. It was set in the Great Hall, built almost twenty years before to accommodate large gatherings. Now the whole family, children, as well, had worked to decorate it and make it beautiful for the party. When Dana looked in, Jack Cordell and Sandra were perched on stepladders busy hanging Christmas swags with glossy green foliage and dozens of gold and scarlet baubles. Even the dais where the band would be playing was decorated with a semicircle of "snow"-tipped Christmas trees in pots flashing tiny white lights. Like so many stars. Everything that could be tied with a big gold-trimmed ribbon was tied. The children loved it; all the Christmas songs were played constantly, they hugged one another exuberantly, thrilled they would be allowed to stay up until nine-thirty. No later. They had to be in bed and fast asleep before Santa Claus began patrolling the station.

Dana chose a beautiful gold dress to wear to the party. Actually it was her bridesmaids dress from a friend's wedding. She had brought it with her thinking it was suitable for the Christmas ritual. The bodice was gold lace, the calf-length full skirt lustrous taffeta. She even had a small jewelled headpiece to catch up her hair at the crown. She had debated arranging her hair in a coil

then decided to leave it out. She couldn't fail to be aware
Logan found her long hair exciting. Searing relief still
washed over her at the memory of Melinda's "confes-
sion." Maybe it was Melinda's peculiar way of letting
her know she loved her. And it vindicated Jimmy who
could have lived such a different life.

Dana was almost ready to go downstairs and join the
others when someone came to her door. Almost certainly
Ainslie. Alice, she knew was with the children, every
last one of them radiant with happiness and excitement.

"Logan!" She stared up at him, her limbs melting,
almost literally because she had to hold on to the door-
jamb. "You look wonderful." It wasn't as much a com-
pliment as a plain statement of fact. He was wearing a
white dinner jacket with his black dress trousers, a white
pin-tucked shirt adorned by a blue silk tie.

He smiled at her, his handsome face a little taut.
"Thank you. A man does his best, but no one will be
able to match you. You look breathtaking." His blue
eyes moved over her with an almost unbearable pleasure.
"May I come in for a moment?"

"Of course." She took a deep breath, held it, convinced from the underlying seriousness of his demeanour
matters between them would come to a head. She heard
herself asking, almost shakily, "Everything's all right,
isn't it?"

"Fine." He seemed to come out of a slight reverie.
He was standing in the centre of the room, now he turned
to face her directly. "I have something to give you before we go down. I hope you'll honour me and wear it
tonight. But first I wanted to thank you from the bottom
of my heart for everything you've done for my family."

Dana pressed her hands together, fighting an irresistible impulse to weep. "Oh, Logan, you don't have
to say this," she implored.

"I do." His reply was harsh, self-judgemental. "I

want to thank you for your great loving kindness to Alice. For the way you have supported Ainslie and Sandra. The way you tried to help Tyler through the difficult times. I even admire your loyalty to Melinda even when we both know she doesn't deserve it. You've been strong through the tragedy that has engulfed us all.''

"Please, Logan," Dana begged. "You needn't say any more. Alice and I are blood kin. I've had all my efforts rewarded. I have love and I have enduring friendships.''

"You must let me finish, Dana," he said inexorably. "I want you to forgive me. I want you to forgive me for ever having doubted you. No matter what I've *said*, I knew you wouldn't fly in the face of honour. I knew you would never betray anyone. Even before Melinda's conscience attack, I *knew*." He paused, admitting, "I do have a hard streak at times. Put it down to the fact I'm not a man who finds it easy to hand over his heart. And yet I have. I love you." His blue eyes blazed. "I love you body and soul." He reached out and very tenderly stroked her cheek. "You fill me with the most beautiful feelings I've ever known. You bring me sweetness and character, dazzling joy. Even when you wring my emotions dry, you're my shining hope. I just can't go on like this. I need a resolution.''

"Oh, so do I!" Dana responded. It came out like a vow. "You're everything to me, Logan. I don't *have* a life unless we're together.''

"But your career?" He cupped her face between his hands, held it still. "I can't let you go off and leave me. I couldn't bear it.''

"Not even for a short time?" she asked in a profoundly happy voice.

His mouth twisted into a wry smile. "How much time are we talking exactly?''

Dana smiled, linked her slender arms behind his neck. "What's wrong with coming with me sometimes? We would manage. I have a lifetime's work out here. A thousand ideas. Anyway, you have some explaining to do. You haven't actually asked me to marry you."

"Okay." He moved her in very close. "Marry me, Dana Barry." He bent to drop multiple kisses on her lips, feather-light so as not to disturb her make-up, the tip of his tongue just entering her mouth. "You know you've always loved me."

All of a sudden she *was* crying, though her heart was filled with boundless joy. This was one of the great moments of life.

"Darling, please don't." His voice was a mixture of amusement, dismay and indulgence. "You simply have no idea what it does to me. And we have to go downstairs."

"I just *need* to..." Dana made a valiant effort to blink back teardrops.

"Here." He removed a beautiful monogrammed handkerchief from his pocket and dabbed very gently at her cheeks. "I can't tell you how much *I* need to give you everything you want." His vibrant voice rang with a passionate seductiveness. "Dana, darling," he warned, "if you don't stop we might have to forget the party altogether."

"No... No... " She lifted her head, paused, inhaled a long deep breath. "Do I look all right?" She stared up so sweetly into his face. Glorious, radiant, she brought a lump to his throat.

"Perfect."

A great sense of peace was moving over him. An intensely felt joy. This was Christmas Eve. He had asked the woman he loved to marry him. Now he reached into his breast pocket and produced a diamond ring so exquisite Dana gasped.

"This is for you, my love," he murmured, gently, so gently, taking her hand. "It belonged to my mother. It was her engagement ring and it's one of my greatest treasures. My father gave me all my mother's jewellery when I was only a boy. 'This is for *your* wife, Logan,' he said to me, and there were tears in my proud father's eyes. 'This is bonding us all together. Past and future. This is keeping our heritage alive.' I've never offered this ring to anyone but you, Dana. I believe now that was the forces of destiny at work. If you would like something else, something of your own choice, you have only to say."

The light in his eyes brought back the tears. She felt for a moment there were other presences in the room. Loving presences who gave them their blessing. "Put it on my finger, Logan," she invited with absolute reverence. "Put it where it belongs."

MEN at WORK

All work and no play?
Not these men!

January 1999
SOMETHING WORTH KEEPING by Kathleen Eagle

He worked with iron and steel, and was as wild as the mustangs that were his passion. She was a high-class horse trainer from the East. Was her gentle touch enough to tame his unruly heart?

February 1999
HANDSOME DEVIL by Joan Hohl

His roguish good looks and intelligence drew women like magnets, but Luke Branson was having too much fun to marry again. Then Selena McInnes strolled before him and turned his life upside down!

March 1999
STARK LIGHTNING by Elaine Barbieri

The boss's daughter was ornery, stubborn and off-limits for cowboy Branch Walker! But Valentine was also nearly impossible to resist. Could they negotiate a truce...or a surrender?

Available at your favorite retail outlet!

MEN AT WORK™

If you enjoyed what you just read,
then we've got an offer you can't resist!

Take 2 bestselling
love stories FREE!

Plus get a FREE surprise gift!

My Secret Admirer

Savor the magic of love
with three new romances
from top-selling authors
**Anne Stuart,
Vicki Lewis Thompson and
Marisa Carroll.**

My Secret Admirer is a unique collection
of three brand-new stories featuring passionate
secret admirers. Celebrate Valentine's Day with
these wonderfully romantic tales that are
ideally suited for this special time!

Available in February 1999 at your favorite retail outlet.

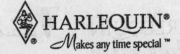

HARLEQUIN®
Makes any time special ™

**Turn up the heat
this March with**

Mallory
Rush

L O V E
P L A Y

From the author of the sexiest
Harlequin® book ever...

Whitney Smith was the classic good girl. But now
the Fates had conspired against her and for once in
her life she was going to live....

Desperately falling in love, Whitney learned about
passion and fire, not caring if she stepped too close
to the flames...until Eric wanted one thing Whitney
couldn't give him—forever!

Look for *Love Play* this February 1999,
available at your favorite retail outlet!

HARLEQUIN®
Makes any time special ™